CUMBRIA LIBRARIES

3 8003 04770 8979

STL

Cumbria

KT-491-520

Libraries

SEATON

06/17

8 - JUN 20

24 FEB 2020

WITHDRAWN

0 3 APR 2018
0 1 NOV 2018
2 3 AUG 2019
- 5 SEP 2019

Please return/renew this item by the last date shown.
Library items may also be renewed by phone on
030 33 33 1234 (24hours) or via our website

www.cumbria.gov.uk/libraries

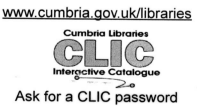

Cumbria Libraries

CLIC
Interactive Catalogue

Ask for a CLIC password

FREAKY & FEARLESS

Bazookas for Beginners

ROBIN ETHERINGTON

ILLUSTRATED BY JAN BIELECKI

Piccadilly
PRESS

FOR TILDA — WITHOUT WHOM NONE OF
WHAT FOLLOWS WOULD EXIST — **RE & JB**

First published in Great Britain in 2017 by
PICCADILLY PRESS
80–81 Wimpole St, London W1G 9RE
www.piccadillypress.co.uk

Text copyright © Robin Etherington, 2017
Illustrations copyright © Jan Bielecki, 2017

All rights reserved.
No part of this publication may be reproduced, stored or transmitted
in any form by any means, electronic, mechanical, photocopying or
otherwise, without the prior written permission of the publisher.

The right of Robin Etherington and Jan Bielecki to be identified as
Author and Illustrator of this work has been asserted by them in
accordance with the Copyright, Designs and Patents Act, 1988

This is a work of fiction. Names, places, events and incidents are
either the products of the author's imagination or used fictitiously. Any
resemblance to actual persons, living or dead, is purely coincidental.

A CIP catalogue record for this book is available from the British
Library.

ISBN: 978-1-8481-2584-1
also available as an ebook

1

Printed and bound by Clays Ltd, St Ives Plc

MIX
Paper from
responsible sources
FSC® C018072

Piccadilly Press is an imprint of Bonnier Zaffre Ltd,
a Bonnier Publishing company
www.bonnierpublishing.com

CHAPTER 1

A FREAKY INVITATION

Simon Moss closed the comic and felt a shiver run up his spine. Swapping comics with his best friend Whippet Willow was a dangerous game to play and, he had to admit, he was feeling pretty spooked at that moment, but while the latest issue of **FREAKY** was undoubtedly full to bursting with shocks and scares, it was NOT the cause of his distress.

Not by a long way.

The real cause was four years old, three and a half feet tall, covered in peanut butter and currently sitting outside the cupboard beneath the stairs. Outside the cupboard in which Simon had been hiding for the past hour.

There was no escaping it. He was being stalked by his sister, Ruby.

Simon's mum called to him from the kitchen.

'Your toast is going over the fence in five seconds, Simon. Come out and eat your breakfast!'

Simon sighed, opened the door and shivered again. Ruby was sitting facing him with a curious expression on her face. One eyebrow was raised and one eye was squinting. Her lips were pursed. Her nose was wrinkled up. The overall effect made her look as if she'd just stepped in something unpleasant.

She was blocking his path to the kitchen.

'Er, do you mind?' said Simon, but his sister made no attempt to move and continued to stare at him with a face like a chihuahua sucking on a lemon.

Simon shook his head and took a huge step over her. Girls were hard to figure out, he thought. Siblings were pretty hard work. Sisters combined the worst of both. He walked into the kitchen and sat down in front of his cold, cold toast. Before he had even managed to raise the slice to his mouth, Ruby had materialised in the chair opposite.

Enough was enough.

'Ruby, what is wrong with you? Why won't you leave me alone?' said Simon.

'None of that, you two,' said Simon's mum, from the end of the dinner table. The Saturday-morning breakfast ritual was usually performed by Simon's dad, and it was one in which he took great pride — banana pancakes being a regular feature. But that was back *then*. Since Simon's father had left home for a business trip at the beginning of the summer, Saturdays had been different. There were no pancakes for one thing.

Simon blew a loud raspberry at Ruby. It

was a childish gesture but he was a child, so what? He bit angrily into his cold, chewy toast. It was like trying to eat a slipper. In an attempt to wash the toast down, he grabbed his favourite **FEARLESS**-branded mug, raised it to his lips and took a big gulp of his now-stone-cold tea. Simon had been hiding in the cupboard for so long that a skin had formed on the surface. It stuck to his lips. He gagged.

Worst. Breakfast. Ever.

Simon scowled at Ruby. He liked his sister. Loved her, actually. Five weeks ago, Simon had rescued her from the clutches of a monster. He didn't mean a metaphorical monster, like an angry teacher or a class bully, but a living, breathing, snorting, blood-curdling horror that collected noses and hid beneath the town of Lake Shore, skulking in the shadows of the sewers. Simon had eventually found Ruby, assisted

by his neighbour (and best friend) Whippet Willow and their new ally Lucy Shufflebottom – a girl so terrifyingly dangerous she'd made the monster they were chasing look like a kitten. Together the three of them had beaten the beast and saved Ruby. There was a lot more to it, but basically it was the stuff of legends.

Then, two weeks later on a camping trip, the trio had blown up a lightning-spitting winged menace by plugging its mouth with a human skull. Ruby hadn't been there for that particular escapade and she'd seemed pretty normal when he first got home.

But once again, that was *then* and this was *now*. And this *now* had taken to following

him everywhere. Silently, creepily, watching his every move.

Some thanks for saving your skin, thought Simon, and took a second bite of his breakfast, which he regretted even more than the first.

There was a knock at the front door. Simon looked at Ruby. Ruby looked at Simon. Simon and Ruby looked at their mum.

'Get that, would you, Simon, dear?' said Simon's mum.

Ruby smiled for the first time. Simon swallowed and sulkily slouched into the hallway. He'd secretly imagined that being the man of the house in his dad's absence would be pretty cool. Protecting his home and family and calling the shots. But the reality was that his list of chores had grown and he'd had to babysit Ruby a lot. A LOT. Now the summer was almost at an end, with only a week to go before he headed off to his new school. Like most boys his age, Simon wasn't exactly looking forward to being a new kid in the lowest year in a place he didn't know.

However, the summer wasn't over just yet. There was still plenty of adventure to be had, and Simon was hoping like crazy that his last free weekend would be an eventful one. But until he opened the front door, he had no idea *how* eventful.

For there, standing before him and scowling professionally, was a pirate.

A pirate holding a large gold envelope in a larger outstretched hand.

A gold envelope embossed with large bright red letters.

Bright red letters that read:

For the eyes of Master Simon Moss only!
YOUR ATTENDANCE
IS REQUIRED!

CHAPTER 2

AW, SHUCKS ... SNAP

'Um, hello, Captain,' said Simon nervously. 'How are you?'

'Fair to middlin', lad,' said Captain Armstrong, rocking backwards lightly on his good heel and his wooden leg.

'Excellent,' said Simon.

Pause.

'An' . . . er, 'ow be ye?' said the Captain in a strained voice.

'Oh, fine. Yep, all good,' said Simon.

There was another awkward pause, which Simon realised he was going to have to fill if they wanted to get things moving. The Captain was talented at many things, but apparently small talk was not one of them.

'Is that for me?' said Simon, pointing at the envelope.

The Captain looked down at the letter, as if he'd forgotten he was holding it. He snapped back into life.

'Ar, this be your property all right, lad, an' no mistake,' he boomed, then handed him the envelope. Simon held it gently. The gold paper was faintly embossed with tiny comic-book speech bubbles. Simon looked up.

'Kind of you to bring, um, whatever *this* is, Captain. But you could have just posted it.'

The Captain shook his head, causing his moustache and beard to sway from side to side. It was like watching a cat swinging from a tree.

'Rules be rules, Mossy. I got clear instructions, an' they be "'*AND delivered and 'AND delivered only*". But I can't stop, mind. The other DELIVERY 'asn't arrived. It being Saturday an' all, I 'ave to find out what's 'appened. Bad to leave the shop locked up for too long, you know?'

Simon did know. Captain Armstrong — who Simon quite seriously believed was actually, *genuinely* a real-life pirate — ran the Shipshape Shop in town. The shop specialised in all manner of toys, collectibles and novelties, but its most sought-after treasures were the new copies of the **FREAKY** and the **FEARLESS** comics, which went on sale every Saturday morning. This was the 'delivery' in question. If the shop didn't open on time, there would probably be an uprising. A riot.

Or at the very least some pretty serious whinging.

'I'm sorry . . . what is this?' said Simon, looking at the envelope.

'A date with destiny, lad,' said the Captain in a meaningful way. 'Just open 'er up an' see.'

Simon looked from the envelope to the Captain and back again. A thought suddenly occurred to him.

'How did you know where I lived?' asked Simon.

The Captain coughed into his fist.

'Ah, well, er . . . comics! Ar, that be it. Yer address be on the **FEARLESS** comic fan-club list. The fan club I 'elp run, by the way. Not sure anyone knew that, but ye do now!'

Simon thought about this. It sounded believable. But he couldn't shake the feeling that the Captain was hiding something.

It was at that moment that Simon's mum appeared behind him in the doorway.

'Ah, well, you *must* be Mr Armstrong,' she said. 'I've heard so much about you. Simon is a huge fan of your shop. Would you like a cup of tea?'

The Captain doffed his tricorn hat to Simon's mum.

'Apologies, ma'am, I've got to run. I 'ope ye can make it, Simon lad . . . Just . . .

watch 'ow ye go. Ye can reach me at the shop, once you've discussed things with yer mum, of course.'

And with that he spun on his wooden leg and strode away up the drive.

It had been a strange brief encounter.

'That's a *very* realistic pirate costume. Is he going to a party?' asked Simon's mum, before turning her attention to the object Simon was holding. 'What's that?'

Back in the kitchen, a rip and a tear later, and Simon and his mum had their answer. The envelope had been opened and discarded, its contents now held in Simon's feverish grip. It was a letter, handwritten with a fountain pen, judging by the irregular swirls and whirls of the old-fashioned curly lettering. The sentences dancing in front of him were making his heart race.

Words. Words had power.

Not just *what* you say, but *how* you say it.

'How you say what, dear?' asked his mum.

Simon had been speaking his thoughts out loud again. It was a recently acquired habit, and one he wished he could control. It only seemed to happen when he was using his power, or thinking about his power. Words were his strength, but it didn't do to go around sharing all your thoughts, so Simon hurriedly diverted the conversation to more important matters.

'Mum, listen to this. You're not going to believe it. It's from the owners of the **FEARLESS** comic! Apparently they were so impressed with that short story I sent in that they've invited me to a special dinner! At the comic headquarters! As a *prize*!'

Simon's mum raised an eyebrow. Ruby had one eyebrow still raised from before, so she raised the other one for good measure. The change made her look like a startled rabbit caught in the headlights of a truck.

'I remember that story,' said Simon's mum with a smile. 'After the camping trip. Something about a giant stampede, a herd stretching to the horizon, running flat out, with no one knowing why they had started running or where they were running to.

I liked it. It was chilling . . .'

She paused. Thinking.

'But I seem to remember that you didn't win that competition,' she continued.

'No, but it's not about winning, is it? That's what you always tell us,' said Simon.

'*Prizes* are about winning, Simon. You didn't even get a mention in the comic.'

Simon paused mid-thought. His mum was right.

'Either way, *please* can I go? It's not just a dinner . . . you do know where the **FEARLESS** comic headquarters are, don't you?' asked Simon, getting a bit worked up with excitement.

'Where?' said Simon's mum.

'Castle Fearless! *THE* Castle Fearless. The castle in town that no one – no one – has ever been inside. This letter is an invitation to dinner with the *owners*! A tour of the comic empire! This is the stuff of DREAMS!!!'

He was laying it on a little thick, but for good reason.

'When is this dinner?'

'Tonight,' replied Simon, in a very small voice.

'Tonight . . . hmm. Problem is, I'm going to the cinema with Mrs Willow, as you well know. You were *supposed* to be looking after Ruby. I'll have to find a replacement.'

'Danica can do it,' said Ruby instantly, the words spilling from her mouth. Simon turned. Danica Patel was a pretty girl from Simon's old school. She had also recently become rather attached to Whippet. *Why* was anyone's guess, as far as Simon was concerned.

He looked at Ruby. Now it was his turn to frown.

'How do you know Danica?'

'Danica . . . oh yes, I remember her,' said Simon's mum. 'She was the Pied Piper in your school play, Simon. Lovely girl. I think she's done a bit of babysitting for one of my friends.'

'I'm not a baby,' said Ruby, as she tried to stick three biscuits into her mouth at once, biscuits she'd stolen from the tin when their mum wasn't looking.

Simon's mum sighed.

'Oh, very well, Simon. You can go. But I'll need to know—'

'YES, WHATEVER! ANYTHING! EVERYTHING! BRILLIANT – BYE, MUM! YOU'RE THE BEST,' yelled Simon in delight before stuffing the letter back into the envelope, sprinting out of the kitchen, through the front door, down the driveway, along the pavement, and up the next driveway, to number 42 – the blue door of the home of his best friend.

Simon grabbed the St Bernard door knocker and raised it high. He paused. Then he lowered it gently. Memories of almost being trampled beneath a sea of furry feet flooded back. It was an occupational hazard when your friend's mum ran a dog-sitting service, but Simon had made the mistake too many times. No knocking. Pure stealth.

Simon bent down and prised open the letter box, which seemed rather fitting, considering what he had brought to show his friend. He was about to whisper through the flap when a tongue appeared in the gap. It was as large as a steak. Before Simon could react, the tongue flicked out and up and gave him a massive slobbery lick from chin to forehead.

'AGH!' gasped Simon, stumbling backwards, his face dripping with saliva. As he frantically wiped it off, the door opened and there was Whippet, standing before him wearing his favourite black T-shirt emblazoned with a skull. He was also wearing a smile so large it was threatening to push his ears out from behind his unruly mop of black hair and possibly knock them right off his head.

Whippet wasn't usually this happy to be in the outside world, thought Simon.

Unless . . . *eurgh!*

'That better not have been *you*,' said Simon, wiping his face and laughing.

'Haha! Nope, not me. Mossy, meet *Drool*,' said Whippet, and led a huge dog out from behind the door. The animal's mane was thick and black and so long that it practically covered its eyes. Its legs were like four hairy tree trunks. The thing was huge, and the tongue lolling from its mouth confirmed Whippet's story. Simon had been slobbered by a lion!

'What . . . ? What is it?' asked Simon, pointing at the dog.

'*He's* a rare Tibetan Mastiff. He belongs to Mr Liu.' Whippet pulled something from his back pocket. 'And *this* is the craziest bit of news I've ever had to share with you.'

Simon's mouth fell open, almost as wide as Drool's.

Whippet was holding a gold envelope.

'No way,' said Simon in a whisper.

'Way,' said Whippet. 'Wait . . . what? You know what's in here?'

Simon nodded and picked his own letter up from where it had fallen on the driveway.

'Snap. I got an invite for that short story I sent in.'

'The one that didn't win?' said Whippet.

'Yeeees, exactly,' said Simon slowly. 'Hmm. What was *yours* for?'

'Bonus prize. For winning that readers' art competition. My superpower just keeps bringing me luck!'

Ah yes, a word on superpowers.

Simon and Whippet, for no reason either had yet been able to explain, possessed what would normally be described as 'powers'. Simon's had emerged first. At certain times, in certain situations – usually when being attacked by a monster – Simon found his stories had the power to hypnotise an audience. Everyone simply HAD to listen to him. And it didn't stop there. Simon was able to find out details about creatures he'd never even met before. Learn their names. Understand their motives. It was all pretty amazing – the stuff of comic books.

Whippet's power was even harder to fathom. He could bring his drawings to life. Not all the time. (The boys had tried it A LOT since returning from their last chaotic adventure. Sweets, toys, games, bikes . . . They couldn't conjure any useful swag.) But in certain stressful situations, Whippet had given his sketches the power of life. He'd drawn a tub of extra-sticky glue that had helped defeat the Screaming Haggle – a winged demon, which had eventually exploded – not to mention a six-legged mammoth, which had saved their lives.

Yes, six legs. Quite.

The original drawing of the mammoth had been sent into a **FREAKY** readers' art competition and had been awarded first place. Whippet was an amazing artist, so it wasn't really surprising.

Whippet looked from the matching envelope to his friend and his smile grew wider still. Which shouldn't have been medically possible, but it was.

'*Castle . . .*'

'*. . . Fearless!*'

The boys yelled in delight and jumped into the air, punching the sky. They danced a comedy jig on the pavement, yelping and whooping. Drool joined in with a huge bark, which sent the birds flying from the nearby trees. Panting and laughing, the pair headed indoors and out into Whippet's back yard with Drool following obediently. The

Willow family didn't really have a garden. The space behind the house was used as a playground for all the neighbourhood dogs they looked after, and because dogs love to dig and scrabble, it more closely resembled a building site. There were cavernous pits everywhere with piles of mud and dirt in between. Not to mention all the dogs.

Drool waltzed into the seething canine horde, greeted by barks, yips and woofs. Simon and Whippet scrambled up onto the roof of one of the larger kennels to watch the dogs play.

'This trip needs preparation,' said Simon.

'Yeah! Definitely. Did you read the bit at the bottom? *Dress Code: Black tie*. What does that mean?'

'Er, we have to wear black ties?'

Whippet frowned. He was starting to look a little worried. 'It sounds like we're going to a funeral.'

'You only *ever* wear black, so what are you worrying about? But that's not what I meant by getting ready. You know what these things are, don't you?' said Simon, waggling his invitation.

'Invitations?'

'No . . . I mean, yes, but they're not just that. They're our key to getting into LUCY'S house!'

Whippet's eyes widened. 'Of course – Lucy! Do you really think she lives there?

Boy, if it's true then I've got a few questions to ask that little red-haired lunatic . . .'

'Me too,' agreed Simon. 'In particular, I'd like to know if she had something to do with us getting invited in the first place. I didn't win the story competition, but I still got a prize? That's exactly the sort of stunt she'd pull. But why?'

Simon was convinced that Lucy Shufflebottom – the most deadly girl alive – didn't really want the simple pleasure of their company. Simon and Whippet had crossed paths with Lucy twice before, and both monster-fighting meetings had been memorable. The trio had survived perils that would make grown men cry, and that

sort of action forges a special connection between people – an adventurers' bond.

Still, they were not exactly friends. Friends phone each other, meet up, have fun, share music or games, stay over, watch movies, mess about and get up to all sorts of mild (but rarely death-defying) mischief when there are no adults in sight. Lucy *definitely* did not fit into that category. Except the last point. They hadn't seen or heard from her since . . .

The boys knew almost nothing about Lucy except that she was handy with her home-made weapons and gadgets, and that she lived, unbelievably, *inside* Castle Fearless.

'Yeah . . . Lucy *might* be behind it,' said Whippet nervously. 'It is all a bit too good to be true.'

'It's too early for conspiracy theories,' said Simon firmly. 'But we'll keep our eyes open. Now, do you think we should bring something to the castle?'

'Like what?' said Whippet.

'You know, something to show just what sort of dedicated **FEARLESS** fans we are.'

'Hmm. That's a good idea.'

Whippet pulled a biro from his pocket and began to scratch his chin absentmindedly while he pondered the idea. Simon fought back a smile as he realised Whippet was using the wrong end of the pen. He was slowly, without realising it, drawing a small black beard on his chin.

There was no way Simon was going to tell him about THAT just yet. Those sorts of accidental jokes emerge too rarely in life. They need to be savoured.

'A pile of our favourite issues isn't going to do it, Mossy, nor a **FREAKY** T-shirt or even our fan-club membership cards,'

noted Whippet. 'We need to prove we're SUPER-fans. We'd better show them something extra-special – a *What-the-heck-is-that-slice-of-awesome?* something.'

Simon nodded thoughtfully and jumped down from the kennel. 'Okay. I've a bunch of chores to run today, then I'll find proof of our super-fan status. Meanwhile, you call the Shipshape Shop to let the Captain know we're both coming to dinner at the castle

– oh, and pick up today's comics. Then . . . well, then we'll be ready for anything.'

It was a nice sentiment, but Whippet and Mossy could never have prepared themselves for the evening ahead. For how can you truly prepare yourself for the end of the world when you don't even know what *Black Tie* means?

CHAPTER 3

MEANWHILE, ELSEWHERE . . .

This one was bigger than the rest.

Much bigger.

It was all slippery suckers and twisting limbs and impossible to contain. Knuckles would have called it a squid, but that would have given harmless squids the world over a really bad name.

He dodged and rolled away, narrowly avoiding a giant blood-red tentacle as it slammed into the ground nearby. He rose in a crouch, clenched his jaw and felt the tension across his arms and back. He'd been battling this particular fiend for half an hour and it had slowly pushed him right back down the valley. They were getting closer. He wouldn't be able to keep this one out. He could really do with the assistance of T-Rex or Armstrong or . . .

WHAM!

Knuckles flew through the air, the wind knocked from his lungs. The squid thing had tricked him. The first slam was just a distraction, while the real attack had come from a tentacle swung from his blind side. Knuckles tumbled across the grass of the valley floor and came to rest against a large yellow rock.

'Well . . . that's going to leave a mark,' he wheezed.

And it had been for nothing. He'd failed. The squiddy beast was passing through the gap, its body vanishing into thin air. One moment it was there, the next it was gone. Elsewhere, things were about to get freaky.

Knuckles slowly picked himself up, rubbing his badly bruised ribs. He shook his head.

This day was going to get much worse before it got better.

If it got better at all.

CHAPTER 4

THE END OF THE WORLD

Many hours later, when Simon's mountain of chores had finally been completed . . .

As Simon's mum explained – while trying to squeeze him into a shirt that didn't quite fit – *Black Tie* meant a smart jacket, smart trousers and smart shoes. And a bow tie, with black being the colour of choice. Simon's mum had embraced the challenge of smartening him up with enthusiasm.

He'd been made to try on waistcoats and cardigans, a military jacket that had belonged to his grandfather and even a wizard cloak from Halloween! Eventually they'd found an outfit that worked.

Simon stood in the downstairs hall and looked at his reflection in the full-length mirror.

'Thanks for this, Mum,' said Simon, 'seriously.'

'You're very welcome,' she replied, adjusting his bow tie.

She stood back and watched as he shrugged himself into an old school blazer that she'd dyed black that afternoon. She gave him a warm smile.

'You know, you'd make a convincing spy, young man,' said Simon's mum. 'It's a shame your father's not here to see you. That tie belongs to him.'

Simon swallowed. He really did miss his dad. Which was not to say that they'd been out of contact, for Simon had chatted with him daily via a secret email address: fearlessfather@farfaraway.world. His dad loved comics and had wanted to know every last detail of Simon's recent monstrous adventures.

'*I* want to go,' said Ruby, who was sitting at the bottom of the stairs watching Simon getting ready. She did not look happy.

Simon knelt before her. Ruby was pretty incredible for a little sister, a fact he'd overlooked until she'd survived a monster attack and acted like nothing had happened. Thinking about this, he suddenly felt a bit guilty for snapping at her earlier.

'Sorry, Rubes, you can't come to this one. But Danica's coming – she'll keep you entertained.'

Then he leaned in and whispered in Ruby's ear, 'And just so you know, Mum hides the *really* good biscuits in a triangular green tin in the top cupboard behind the boring cereal boxes.'

Ruby poked Simon on the nose. 'Just don't go having any adventures without me. It's not fair,' she huffed.

'So *that's* why you've been following me around,' said Simon. 'Ruby, nothing exciting is going to happen. My adventuring days are over.'

Simon stood up. Ruby gave him a long look.

'What about your trip to Wailing Wood? Danica said you blew up a toilet.'

'That wasn't me!'

'Well, what about falling off a bridge into a river?'

'Shhhh,' Simon hissed, glancing at their mum. 'Okay, that WAS me, but it was an accident.'

'Time to go,' said his mum, interrupting their hushed conversation.

Simon froze. Time to go? He'd only had one thing to remember today . . . and he'd forgotten it. The proof!

Simon vaulted up the stairs three at a time, burst into his bedroom and desperately scanned his shelves. He needed to find something unique. Something truly special.

And there it was, sitting on his highest shelf, still in its original box. His limited edition Knuckles action figure. Knuckles was the biggest hero in the **FEARLESS** comic.

Simon picked up the box and tilted it in the dim light. The figure inside was amazingly detailed. The likeness to the comic drawings was incredible. From beneath the mask of the hero, two green eyes stared back. They were the right shape but the wrong colour. For in the pages of **FEARLESS**, Knuckles's eyes were always blue.

'Only one hundred of these toys left the factory before they discovered they'd

got the eyes wrong. This is the proof we need. Only a SUPER-FAN would have one of these,' whispered Simon, and with the box in one hand he sprinted back downstairs and out the front door.

Whippet was waiting at the end of the driveway. He'd made a pretty good effort to find some suitable clothing. He was wearing black jeans and his ever present skull T-shirt beneath an open black jacket. No tie, but there was a reason for that. Whippet was not alone.

Danica Patel, Whippet's newly acquired number-one fan, was holding a black tie behind her back. To get to it, Whippet was going to have to get *very* close to her. Which was probably the intention, thought Simon.

'Please give it back,' said Whippet.

'You're an *artist*, Whippet,' replied Danica. She flicked her head and her long black hair swished elegantly. She fixed her brown eyes on Whippet. 'You shouldn't fight your destiny. You shouldn't pretend to be something you're not. Never, ever.'

She held the tie out in front of her with contempt, almost as if she was gripping a rotting fish.

'THIS is not *you*,' she said.

Whippet sighed in surrender. 'Fine, okay, I won't wear it. Happy now?'

Danica leaned in towards Whippet. It was a lightning-fast move. Whippet had no time to react and the pair ended up nose to nose. 'No, but I'm getting there,' she said softly. Then she turned and strolled past

Simon, bouncing lightly on her feet. She walked up to his house and to Ruby, who was waiting in the doorway.

Whippet looked stunned, but a small smile had formed on his lips. Simon laughed, which broke his friend's dazed state. He looked extremely embarrassed.

'Right, Mossy, er, let's get to this dinner, yes?' Whippet was in quite a fluster and practically dived into the back of the car.

'You know, I nearly forgot to pick up our proof,' said Simon, waving the action figure in the air. 'Lucky for us I had this beauty sitting on my shelf.'

Whippet froze and the colour drained from his face.

'Oh, no. Mossy, I did a really, really bad thing,' he mumbled. 'Or rather, I didn't. I had to walk the dogs and then Drool ate my pillowcase and . . . and . . . and my pencil collection needed sharpening, and . . . er . . . my legs decided not to work . . .'

'What is it?' said Simon. He was already on edge and Whippet's excuses weren't helping.

'I forgot to pick up our comics!'

The boys stared at one another in silence for a second.

'Mum! Emergency change of plan! Can you drive us to the Shipshape Shop first, please?'

Simon's mum sighed. 'Okay, but no

lingering. It's almost closing time, and I know what you boys are like.'

As it turned out, there was absolutely no possibility of lingering. After parking the car opposite the shop, Simon, his mum and Whippet simply stared out of the window.

There was a screaming, braying mob of children between the car and the Shipshape Shop. The cause of the ruckus was a large crudely painted sign pinned to the front door, which was locked. And bolted. The sign read:

'It's the end of the world . . .' whispered Whippet weakly.

'I'm getting that feeling, yeah,' said Simon.

As they watched, Ben Chubb, Luke Gristle, Emma Skettle and little Nate Rumble wrenched a rubbish bin from the ground and charged towards the shop, yelling a battle cry. The crowd around them was chanting, *We're going in! We're going in! We're going IN!*

Captain Armstrong had once told Simon that the doors were carved from the hip bone of a foul underwater monstrosity called the *Terrorem Marianas*, a fishy beast that lived in the deepest sea trench on

Earth. Because of the immense underwater pressure on the monster, it had evolved until its bones were believed to be the strongest substance known to humankind.

As Ben, Luke, Emma and Nate quickly discovered.

Their ill-advised charge swiftly ended when the rubbish bin crumpled like a crushed tin can and all four kids slammed head first into the entrance. They slid in slow motion down the undamaged doors until they lay in a bruised heap.

'Right, I think we've seen quite enough,' said Simon's mum as she drove slowly away.

Simon and Whippet turned to gaze out the rear window.

'I'm getting a bad feeling, Mossy. No comics? How can there be NO comics? There's never, *ever* been no comics,' said Whippet miserably.

They watched as Ben and the other children picked themselves up and staggered over to join a large group of their friends who were now chanting rather mournfully.

'WHERE ARE OUR COMIIIIIIICS?'
'WE WANT OUR COMIIIIIIICS!'
'GIVE US OUR COMIIIIIIIICS!'

As rallying calls go, it was hardly Shakespeare, but Simon had to admit their cause was just. You simply *do not* stand between a reader and their favoured reading matter.

But somebody was. The question was who? And why?

CHAPTER 5

HOW TO MEET YOUR HEROES

The rest of the drive passed in silence, until they pulled up to the immense wrought-iron gates of Castle Fearless, which, as always, were shut tight. Simon wanted to be dropped off then and there, but his mum insisted on making sure the boys arrived safely and that everything was above board before she left. After all, no one actually knew who lived in the castle. Except for Lucy, of course.

As they peered out of the windows, all twelve of the security cameras fixed atop the wall turned to face them, tracking from one passenger to the next.

'Creepy,' muttered Simon's mum.
'Clever,' noted Simon.
'Cooooooool,' breathed Whippet.

There was a pause, then a clunk and a clink. And then, ever so slowly, the gates swung inwards, opening before them. The car crunched up the gravel driveway until they came to a halt outside the front of the castle itself. The group climbed out and took in their surroundings. To Simon it was like landing on the moon. He was blazing a trail, standing where no child had stood before.

Again, except for Lucy.

Somewhere a bell sounded. *Bong* after *Bong* after *Bong*. It sounded muffled and distant.

'This place is weird,' commented Simon's mum, staring up at the building. 'It's like no castle I've ever seen.'

Simon agreed that it must look strange, at least to anyone unused to reading **FEARLESS**. There was just so much of it. Massed crenellations, turrets and castellations rising high above them. Windows upon windows, and balconies overlooking each other. Covered walkways strung between distant towers that soared above the mountain of bricks and mortar like sunflowers on a desert plain.

But this was the home of a comic empire. *Weird* was probably the intended design.

There was a light cough. Simon, his mum and Whippet suddenly realised that they had company. Standing in the front portico was an elderly gentleman. He was tall and thin, with a shock of silver-grey hair parted to one side and a small, groomed white beard that clung to the bottom of his pointed chin like a shiny arrowhead. He was dressed in an immaculate red dinner jacket and a frilly-fronted white shirt, complete with a deep red bow tie and matching cummerbund. Simon suddenly felt extremely underdressed and a little confused. The man's tie wasn't even black!

'Huh,' said Simon, 'I guess I thought Lucy might be here to greet us.'

Whippet leaned in to his friend. He

raised a biro in front of Simon's eyes and gave it a wiggle.

'Lucy or no Lucy, this guy's beard reminds me – I want a *word* with you later,' he whispered.

The old man stood as still as a statue. Simon's mum decided to take the initiative and led the boys towards the entranceway.

'Hello, I'm Simon's mother. I just wanted to make sure the boys arrived safely. You can never be too careful, eh?'

'Oh, you can be, my dear,' said the old man, 'but it takes a lot of planning and a LOT of resources. Which I have, by the way.'

His voice was lighter

than Simon had expected, and there was a mischievous twinkle in his eye. Simon liked him instantly. He reminded him a bit of his dad.

'Welcome, young masters, to Castle Fearless, the ancestral home of the comic universe bearing the same name. Tonight I will be your host for a unique experience, the first of its kind. Select areas of the castle are yours to explore; the treasures within, yours to examine at your leisure. I feel confident in saying that once you step through these doors you will find it *extremely* hard to leave.'

Simon and Whippet grinned at each other. This was getting better and better.

'That all sounds wonderful,' said Simon's mum, 'and excuse my bluntness . . . but *who* are you?'

The old man raised an eyebrow.

'Me? Why I am Ernie Shufflebottom, of course. Master of the castle and the sole owner of **FEARLESS**.'

'Shufflebottom?' said Whippet.

'Yes. Of course the name is familiar to you. I believe you know my granddaughter.'

And the first piece of the puzzle fell into place.

'So Lucy really does live here?' asked Simon.

Ernie raised a hand and stroked his chin. He paused before speaking.

'Yes, Lucy and I occupy the same castle, but we inhabit different wings. She does her thing, whatever that is, and I do mine – which is writing comic stories that make the world gasp and giggle. Aside from being the owner of **FEARLESS**, I am also the head writer.'

Simon's eyes widened. 'Did you write

Red's Revenge?' he said breathlessly.

'Yes,' said Ernie, with a satisfied smile.

'What about *Batty Beasts*?' said Whippet, rubbing his hands in joy.

'That too,' said the old man.

'How about *Knuckles and Duster*?' said Simon, clutching his boxed figure a little tighter.

'One of my personal favourites, and, yes, I did. Now, if we're going to attempt to list all my achievements, I suggest we do it indoors, with a glass of something bubbly and an hors d'oeuvre or three.'

He gestured towards the doors and the boys bounded forward, desperate to get inside. As they passed him, Ernie turned his gaze to Simon's mum.

'Madam, I bid you a most splendid evening. Rest assured, Simon and Whippet will be taken care of. As of this moment, these two boys are my number-one concern.'

Simon's mum reminded them that she'd be at the cinema later with her phone on silent, but to call if they needed her. Then she waved goodbye, climbed back in the car and drove away.

The boys entered the castle and Ernie gripped the iron handles of the double doors and began to pull them shut.

At the last possible moment, a smudge of black dropped from just above the portico roof and landed on four small feet – feet shaped like a monkey's hands – right where the boys had been standing. It darted between the doors just as they closed with a thud.

Gubbin had entered the building.

CHAPTER 6

THE LIBRARY OF WOW

Ernie Shufflebottom was true to his word. On a small table beside the front door sat a tray. On it was a plate of mini sausage rolls and three glasses. Two of the glasses were filled with lemonade, which the boys eagerly accepted. The third held champagne, which Ernie used to silently toast Simon and Whippet. Everyone grabbed a snack, chinked glasses and then they were off.

Naturally the boys had no idea where they were going, so they simply concentrated on trying to keep up, which was harder said than done. For an old man, Ernie could move at quite a pace and had a tendency to nip round blind corners without warning. If that wasn't bad enough, there were a lot of distractions demanding their attention.

Every wall and hall the boys navigated was adorned with tapestries, weapon racks, pennants and shields emblazoned with crests, coats of arms and mottos. Not to mention lots and lots of cool comic swag.

Ernie stopped at an alcove. Mounted on the wall was a gigantic red fist, with a yellow lightning bolt painted across the clenched fingers.

'Does this ring any bells?' he asked with a smile.

'It's . . . It's the Hand of Tregor,' said Whippet breathlessly. 'A floating hand that sought justice while hunting, eternally, for its missing body . . . a classic **FREAKY** tale!'

'Very good,' said Ernie with a nod.

He spun on his heel.

'And what about this?'

Simon turned to study the corridor wall opposite. A cloak was wrapped around a mannequin. It showed signs of having been burnt, torn, mauled, perforated, stained, glued, hacked and chewed.

'Oh, wow . . . that's . . . that's Cloak from *Shroud of the Damned*. A blessing and a curse to all who wore it, for although they would know true power, they'd also meet a most grisly end. That story was the only one ever to appear in both **FREAKY** AND **FEARLESS**!'

Ernie nodded with something like pride, then set off again. They passed countless other treasures that Simon would have dearly loved to stop at for a better look, but Ernie's pace was relentless. On and on they wove, silently, through a seemingly endless maze of rooms and corridors, until finally their host stopped before a stone archway. The sudden halt took Whippet entirely by surprise. He tried to slow himself, but unfortunately the movement began on a rug.

A rug on a polished wooden floor.

The boy and the rug skidded past Simon and Ernie at some speed. Whippet made a desperate sideways grab for something to stop his forward motion. He chose poorly. Whippet and the sliding rug *and* the suit of armour he'd lunged for continued onwards. The suit of armour seemed to be reaching out, trying to grab something to stop them both.

Unfortunately it also chose poorly.

Boy, rug, armour and ancient tapestry slid into the next room.

There was a loud thud from inside.

Simon and Ernie
peered through the doorway
to where a dazed Whippet was
struggling to sit upright.

Then Simon heard another sound and looked upwards. Balanced high, high above Whippet, teetering and tottering on a shelf, was a grand blue vase. It lurched. It wobbled. It wibbled.

Then it fell. Simon held his breath.

But there was no smash or crash. Miraculously Whippet had caught the vase!

Ernie smiled.

'That was something I'd have written, once upon a time, but the vase would have landed on his head. Might have made the scene longer and placed a few more comedy objects in his path. A tin of paint. A monkey. Some carol singers, perhaps,' he mused. 'Is your friend always like this?'

'If I said no, I'd be fibbing through my teeth,' said Simon with an apologetic smile.

'We wouldn't want that. Lies are so . . . consuming. *Addictive* might be a better word,' said Ernie. He fell silent. 'Well, let's make sure no harm's been done.'

They found Whippet kneeling among the scraps of armour.

'Are you okay, pal?' asked Simon, helping his friend to his feet. Whippet looked around in shock.

'Mossy . . . Mossy, look where we are . . . Look at them all, just look . . .'

Simon looked up and took in the room around him. His eyes grew wide, the pupils expanding.

'I thought you might have that reaction,'

said Ernie, placing the miraculously undamaged pot on a small table and strolling over to the nearest shelf. He ran a finger along its contents. The sound was like a playing card stuck between the spokes of a speeding bike.

The room they were standing in was circular and stretched up and up, almost three times as tall as Ernie. The shelves wound round and round the room like a continual orange peel, lining the walls from ground to ceiling, which was saying something as the upper shelves were so high they could only be accessed via a special ladder on wheels.

Ernie pulled an item at random from the shelf beside him. It was covered by a plastic protective bag. He slid the object from its clear wallet and began flicking through the pages as he spoke.

'This, my young friends, is the library.

Or the Library of WOW, as it was dubbed by young Lucy. It contains every single issue of **FEARLESS** that has ever been published. All 2,291 copies of the ongoing series, plus alternative covers, rarities, annuals, spinoffs, collected trades and experimental issues.'

Ernie's eyes glazed over for a second as he looked up from the comic and scanned the room.

'It's quite something, is it not? A whole library of comics in mint condition. An unrivalled collection. Peerless. Priceless.'

Whippet was almost shaking with excitement. Simon couldn't blame him.

'And not just **FEARLESS**,' said Ernie theatrically, pointing over their heads. 'The room also contains all 2,170 copies of **FREAKY**. The comics may be rivals, but they belong together. A little like peanut butter and jam.'

Ernie returned the comic to its sleeve

and placed it back in the correct position on the shelf.

'Now, dinner will be served, promptly, in one hour. I suppose I could continue the castle tour . . . Or perhaps you would rather stay here and—'

'LIBRARY, LIBRARY, LIBRARY,' the boys yelled in unison.

Ernie let out a single laugh. It was a small coughed bark of a sound, like a bullet fired from a silenced gun.

'Very well. The library it is. But just one hour. Then I shall come back to collect you. Be sure to return every issue to its designated spot, yes?'

And with that, Ernie Shufflebottom, founder of the **FEARLESS** empire, strode out of the room, and Simon and Whippet got down to the business of having the time of their lives.

Simon decided to peruse the great

collection from the beginning, in sequence, starting with the very first issue. He studied the room. Where did the series begin? There did not appear to be any form of numbering visible on the wooden shelves and, as the room was entirely circular, the start could be anywhere. While Simon pondered the puzzle, Whippet began pulling out issues at random, an expression of sheer delight spreading across his face with each new discovery.

'Wow . . . Mossy, check out **FREAKY**

issue 2001! It's got a 3D hologram glitter-covered lenticular pop-up cover!'

Simon grinned. Whippet ran anticlock-wise round the room, stopping at another random spot in the same row.

'**FEARLESS** number 1854! A scratch-and-sniff special!'

Whippet flicked quickly through the pages. He stopped, scratched at a picture, gave a big sniff, then reared back in utter disgust.

'Gah . . . You do not – do NOT – want to smell that episode of *Gary Garbage*! The nappy attack is EXTREMELY realistic . . .'

Simon laughed and snapped his fingers. Whippet had accidentally spotted the pattern. The comics were ordered in a slanting circle. Each circled row contained an uninterrupted run of comics, **FREAKY** and **FEARLESS** combined. Testing his theory,

Simon grabbed a comic from the lower row. The number was higher. So the first-ever comic, **FEARLESS** issue #1, must be high up, right near the ceiling.

Simon walked to the ladder that was propped against the shelves. Only now did he realise that it was attached to metal runners, runners that looped in a full circle. The ladder could slide left or right. Simon scampered to the top and plucked a nearby comic. Issue 63.

Ooooh, so close.

'Hey, Whippet, give me a push, would you?' he called down.

Whippet dropped his comic on the randomly selected pile beside him and walked over to the base of the ladder. He grinned upwards.

'A push, Mossy? Whatever you say, buddy,' he chuckled, grabbing the rungs. 'THIS is for the beard trick you pulled earlier! It took me ages to get those pen marks off my face!'

And with that, Whippet shoved the ladder with all his might, sending it whizzing around (and around and around) the room. Simon clung on for his life. As the ladder hurtled in a circle his legs flew out horizontally behind him. But Whippet's revenge didn't have quite the desired effect. Simon was less scared than *excited* by this improvised roller coaster. He let out a whoop of delight as he shot past his best friend for

the fourth time in about ten seconds.

Simon's undoing came about as he tried to slow himself down. He grabbed hold of a shelf, was yanked off the ladder and tumbled to earth in a shower of comics.

High above, balanced on the shelf where the blue vase had once lived, Gubbin allowed himself a smile.

Down below, Whippet ran over to check that his friend was all right.

'Sorry, Mossy, I did not see that coming,' said Whippet apologetically, lifting a section of shelf from his friend's leg.

'Urgh . . . me neither! What a mess we've made. First that suit of armour, and now look at the . . .'

For the second time that evening Simon's words froze in his mouth.

Sitting in his lap, impossibly, lying on top of the scattered comics . . . was **FEARLESS** #1.

More incredible still was the cover. A lone figure, standing on the deck of a burning ship, flame-licked sails billowing behind him, his feet atop the stunned bodies of countless enemies.

A lone pirate. THE lone pirate, actually.

'That looks like—' began Whippet.

'It is,' said Simon. 'I'd recognise that old sea dog anywhere!'

It was, unmistakably, Captain Armstrong. The resemblance was uncanny. It was like staring at a photograph. Whippet scratched his head. Then his eyes widened and he ran back to his pile of randomly plucked comics, which had somehow avoided Simon's fall.

Simon knelt amidst the carnage. He was confused, to put it mildly. How was this possible?

'I don't get it. Maybe . . . Maybe they used Armstrong for inspiration, but . . . but this was over forty years ago! This drawing looks *identical* to OUR Captain NOW. Just how old IS he?'

Whippet was scrabbling among the comics like a dog digging up a bone.

'Where did I see it? *Where? WHERE?!*'

Simon stood, the Armstrong story open in his hands on a double-page, ship-to-ship battle. The strip was called *Captain*

Strongarm. The similarity in names wasn't even subtle.

'YES! I knew it! Mossy, this is getting freaky.'

Whippet stretched out and handed Simon another old comic. The issue number on the cover showed that this one had to be at least thirty years old.

They both stared at the colourful picture splashed across the front. '*Packed with Prehistoric Peril!*' read the legend. And who was dishing out the peril, posing on the back of a swooping pterodactyl, his wooden club held aloft in a hand the size of a baked ham?

Why, none other than their very own caveman camp leader.

'T-Rex . . .' they whispered inshocked unison.

CHAPTER 7

DINNER IS SERVED

Silence descended on the room.

Simon pulled his phone from his pocket and checked the time. This new weirdness was going to have to wait. 'Ernie will be coming back to collect us soon and we've a lot of tidying to do. First, we get this place in order, *then* we officially freak out!'

And that's what they did. Their allotted

hour in the Library of WOW seemed to pass by in the flick of a comic. What with replacing the shelf, arranging the comics back in the right order and rebuilding the suit of armour, the boys had just got everything neat again when their grand host swept back into the room.

He looked around the library with an expression of barely contained surprise.

'Everything looks as it should. I'm shocked. Lucy once made a small fort out of issues 982–1765, which was . . . irritating. Congratulations, boys. You've exceeded my extremely low expectations.'

Simon shot Whippet a quick smile. Whippet mimed wiping his brow in relief.

'All these appetising treats for the eyeballs must have stirred quite a hunger, I reckon. Well, dinner is served, gentlemen. This way, if you please.'

Simon hurriedly picked up his Knuckles action figure. It would have been pretty much the perfect moment to show it, but before Simon could react they were away again. Ernie led the boys out of the library entrance and along a strange corridor. It was neither straight nor curved, but instead was made up of short sections that kept turning to the right at intervals, as if following the outline of a geometric shape. A square? A pentagon? An octagon? Simon hadn't been counting the turns so he had no idea. He felt slightly travel sick.

Actually, thought Simon, it wasn't travel sickness, it was hunger. The sausage rolls they'd eaten were long forgotten and he found himself looking forward to a hearty dinner.

He was therefore pleased

when at last the corridor ended at a large set of open double doors. The boys traipsed after Ernie as he entered the room and an aged butler appeared from the shadows to draw the doors shut behind them. Simon gulped. To call this space a 'room' was rather selling it short. It was a dining hall the size of a football field. The walls rose high above Simon and Whippet. From the furthest summit of the ceiling hung three huge chandeliers, filled with hundreds of candles. A gentle breeze from somewhere

in the room caused the flames to flicker and dance, their illumination bouncing lightly around the voluminous space.

Simon was beginning to feel a little out of his depth and it only got worse as they approached the dining table, a vast slab of oak reaching across the hall like a section of motorway. Four place settings had been laid. Two facing each other in the centre, and one at each end. Ernie gestured for the boys to take the central spots, as he headed for a large ornate chair at the head of the table.

'Oh boy . . .' said Whippet under his breath.

Oh boy, indeed. Simon had never seen so many different pieces of cutlery. He

recognised that there were forks, knives and spoons, but that was where the good times ended. There were things laid on the table in front of him that he'd never even seen before, let alone knew how to use.

They sat down and Simon placed his Knuckles figure on the floor beside his chair. He wasn't sure if he should mention it during the meal or save it as a talking point for after dinner. Either way, Simon guessed it could wait a little longer.

Whippet picked up one curio at random and eyed it suspiciously. It looked like a weapon that an Orc might use to gouge out an opponent's brain in the heart of battle!

'What's the matter, *Freaky*?' called a voice from deep in the shadows at the far end of the table. 'Never seen a pair of SNAIL tongs before? Yum, yum, yum.'

Whippet turned white. Then green. He dropped the tongs. His cheeks puffed out. Simon covered his face in preparation for the worst.

A peal of laughter rang around the cavernous hall. 'You boys are a gift that just keeps on giving.' It was a voice that Simon

recognised only too well. Lucy Shufflebottom leaned forward into the light, elbows on the table.

'LUCY!' yelled Simon.

Both boys jumped up and raced to greet their friend. Knuckle bumps were shared, high fives exchanged, and three excited voices hurriedly talked over one another until a cough and a raised eyebrow from Ernie encouraged them to take their places at the table once again.

'Are you joining us for dinner?' asked Simon, with genuine delight in his voice. He really had grown to like the tiny lunatic.

'Your powers of deduction are as sharp as ever, Simon,' said Lucy, with the slightest of smiles.

'Snails . . .' moaned Whippet miserably, his attention having returned to the strange utensil lying before him.

'Snails,' intoned the butler, who had somehow managed to materialise behind Whippet's chair to place a strange bowl upon his place mat.

There was no getting around it. The bowl was full of snails. Actual snails. In their shells.

The green returned to Whippet's cheeks.

Simon turned to see Ernie give a small smile before plucking a cooked snail from its shell with his own tongs and popping it in his mouth.

'I am as surprised as you both are to see young Lucy here. I can only imagine the presence of you two has something to do with it.'

Lucy shrugged, as if that explained everything.

'I have some questions, Mr Shufflebottom,' said Simon, slowly pushing his chair back from the table so as to distance himself from the first course – which he could swear was still moving.

'As do I, Simon, but please, do go first,' said Ernie in reply.

'Everyone knows this is called Castle Fearless, and it's the **FEARLESS** HQ, but unless I've been misreading my comics all these years, you also make **FREAKY**. Am I right?'

There was a pause. Lucy took the opportunity to flick a snail with her tongs. It bounced off Whippet's head, causing the nervous boy to yelp in fear. Ernie shot her a look.

'You are a bright boy, Master Moss,' said Ernie. 'How did you work that out?'

'I'd suspected it for a while. Some of the art looks similar for one thing. And that got me thinking, Where is **FREAKY** made? In fact, where do *any* of the writers and the artists come from? I've never seen anyone leave this place. Do they live in the castle?' asked Simon.

Ernie leaned back in his chair.

'Impressive. It feels entirely right to share a secret this profound with one so young: Simon, there are *no* other writers.

There never has been. There is also only one artist. He is a . . . difficult man. A strange man. Perhaps even a dangerous man. I worry that a lifetime spent drawing monsters and mayhem might have driven him mad. I'm really not sure *where* he gets his ideas from. Unfortunately, he's informed me he's busy tonight so will be unable to join us.'

Whippet spun in his seat to face Ernie. 'Wait . . . One artist? *ONE?!'*

Ernie placed his cutlery carefully on his now empty plate, which promptly vanished, the old butler squirrelling the dirty crockery away into the darkness. Simon and Whippet's untouched dishes had also been cleared.

'**FREAKY** and **FEARLESS** are drawn by one artist, yes. My long-time associate Buster Brown.'

'But that's . . . that's . . .' began Whippet.

'Impossible?' suggested Simon.

'Incredible!' corrected Whippet with a slightly manic grin.

'Yes, I suppose we *are* rather,' said Ernie, with absolutely no false modesty.

The main course appeared, deft hands laying the plates efficiently and silently. Ernie smiled mischievously at the offering.

'Ah, squid! My favourite. Extra suckers too, Jeffrey. Oh, how you spoil us.'

Simon looked at the thing writhing in front of him. It *could* have been a squid . . . or an octopus . . . or some

unnamed horror from the deep. Whatever it was, it appeared to be smiling. Or passing gas. Neither made for an appetising prospect. Whippet's face was growing more colourful by the minute.

'I hate squid,' whispered Whippet miserably.

Lucy appeared to be entirely unfazed by the meal. She wasn't eating, but she wasn't reacting either. She was just staring down the length of the table at her grandfather, an unreadable expression on her face. For a moment, Simon wondered what it must be like to grow up in a castle.

'My turn now,' said Ernie, tucking a napkin in his collar. 'What do you two boys know about the *rumours*?'

'Rumours?' echoed Simon.

'Monsters and bogeymen on the loose in the town. That sort of thing. I've been hearing all sorts of fantastical nonsense about beasts and birds and who knows what.'

Simon was unsure how he should proceed. If any adult was well placed to help them get to the bottom of the recent mysteries in Lake Shore, it might be Ernie Shufflebottom. He'd certainly be open to the possibility of weirdness. His life had been spent making comics! Surely he would believe them.

But he was Lucy's grandfather. If they were going to share their secrets, the truth should come from her. Judging from Lucy's silence, she didn't seem all that keen on the idea.

'I've heard some of those stories too,' said Simon, treading carefully, 'but they're probably just a joke. A hoax. There's no such thing as monsters . . . right?'

Ernie's tentacle-laden fork paused on its way to his mouth. His eyes locked with Simon's. He seemed to be searching for something.

'My work encourages a certain interest in the peculiar,' said Ernie, slowly, 'but these sorts of urban fantasies rarely have an interesting origin story. A chimp escapes from the zoo one day, and the next thing you know everyone's talking about a thirty-foot-tall goliath that likes to hide in gardens and eat cats. Human beings can be very silly creatures – my partner in crime, Buster, being a good example.'

Simon nodded. The plates had gone again. That disappearing act was almost as unnerving as the contents of the dishes themselves.

There was a scrape of wood on wood as Lucy pushed back her chair and stood up.

'Mossy, Whippet . . . come with me,' she ordered. She led them from the table and the glow of the chandeliers to a side door, hidden in a dark alcove between two large, sombre matching portraits of Ernie. The only difference Simon could spot between the two paintings was the colour of his jacket.

'Lucy, the two young gentlemen haven't finished their dinner. Besides, we've lots more to discuss.'

'No one wants to eat snails or squid, and absolutely NO ONE on the planet wants to finish it off with tapioca pudding! It's like eating frogspawn covered in cream,' said Lucy with a sad shake of the head. 'You *always* serve this up when we have guests. As practical jokes go, even for a comic writer, this one is getting a little old.'

Ernie laughed. 'It's true! I apologise for my cruel sense of humour,' he said with a twinkle in his eye.

Then a bell sounded again. Deep sonorous peals, vibrating through the woodwork around them. It must be the same bell they'd heard outside, but where was it coming from? wondered Simon.

The smile faded from Ernie's lips. He dropped his napkin and rose from the table.

'Young masters, you are excused. Have fun with Lucy, but please confine yourselves to her wing. Castle Fearless can be a hazardous place.'

And to the sound of muffled bells, Ernie swept from the room and was gone.

CHAPTER 8

STAMPEDE

The thundering swarm was spread thick across the line of the horizon.

Hoofs. Claws. Paws. Limbs. Jaws. Two legs or four.

Coming towards him like a panicked tide, rolling heavy as a heatwave.

Onwards. Onwards.

It was only a matter of days. Or a day.

Hours even. He could no longer tell.

Knuckles lowered the binoculars and wiped the sweat from his brow. His mask clung to his mouth. The coat stuck to his skin. Things were definitely heating up.

The trickle of escapees had been hard to control. There had been random leaks, like the giant Squid, which though not ideal were at least manageable. But this . . . this would be a flood on an unimaginable scale. A monster tsunami that would destroy everything in its path, and wreck everything the Guardians had fought so hard and so long to protect.

He turned to face the **PANEL**. Once it had been a beacon of freedom. Of possibility. Now it spelled disaster. Knuckles had disguised it so well it was practically invisible, even from close up, but it still hadn't fooled them all. The Snotticus. The Screaming Haggle. The Squid.

Once again he thought about the boy. How could Simon have known about the stampede?

Knuckles raised his binoculars again. He knew what they were running towards, but he was no closer to learning what they were running *from*.

Hoofs. Claws. Paws. Limbs. Jaws. Two legs or four. A yellow bear-like beast led the thundering swarm as it spread thick across the line of the horizon.

His mask clung to his mouth.

CHAPTER 9

A BRUSH WITH DEATH!

Lucy, Simon and Whippet climbed a wide spiral staircase, chatting animatedly as they went. As usual, Lucy offered no explanation for her absence or silence over the previous weeks, neither did she mention the awesome truth that she was in fact related to one of the creators of both **FREAKY** and **FEARLESS**. Instead she launched into an enthusiastic cross-examination of the boys. Had they been practising their powers? Had they witnessed anything else out of the ordinary? Had they been following the police investigation into the strange happenings in Wailing Wood and the disappearance of amateur birdwatcher Madeline Fortune?

Simon wanted to be helpful, but found it difficult to both concentrate on Lucy's questions and keep track of where they were going. He could find no logic to the construction of Castle Fearless and he found it dizzying. The further into the building they went, the madder it all became. Corridors led on to gantries to hallways to bridges to anterooms to courtyards. Simon knew they were rising slowly, floor by floor, but that was about the only thing he could work out.

And all the while, Gubbin followed secretly, tracking them silently from the shadows.

Halfway through explaining Whippet's failure to bring any of his drawings to 'life' – even something as dull as a picture of an ant – a thought occurred to Simon, and he paused, stopping in the middle of a small indoor bridge.

Yes, an indoor bridge. It was that sort of a place.

'I forgot to ask your grandfather, but what's happened to the latest **FEARLESS**, Lucy? Where are this week's comics?'

Lucy made a steeple from her fingers and tapped the tips of them together thoughtfully.

'I . . . I have absolutely no idea.'

Simon was slightly stunned, but Whippet didn't miss a beat. He slapped his hands over his mouth in mock shock.

'You? Lucy Shufflebottom? YOU don't

have a theory? Call the TV! This is a first! What's the date? I'm noting it down right now . . . this is history in the making! Front-page news!' said Whippet, laughing and scrabbling for his sketchbook.

Lucy reached over, grabbed the book from his hands and threw it off the bridge.

'Hey! I was only messing around. There was no call for that,' protested Whippet hopelessly, and he rushed to the edge.

Lucy ignored him. She paced and chewed on her lip.

'No comics? Hmm . . . this is the first I've heard of it, actually. But . . . Grandfather seems to have been really worried about Buster . . . wait . . . yes . . . *that* makes some sort of sense . . . some sort of horrible, horrible sense . . . *Buster* . . .'

Simon leaned in closer, hanging on Lucy's every word.

In the background Whippet was whimpering. '*My sketchbook* . . .'

Lucy stopped turning in circles. 'Stop being such a drip, Whippet. I'll get you another sketchbook. TWO, if you want. Right now I need you ready for action.'

The distant bell sounded again. Once. Twice. Three times. Simon knew the castle had a bell tower, he'd seen it from the outside, but the sound seemed to be coming from below them. It must be some sort of auditory illusion. With all the crazy architecture, sounds must bounce around in all sorts of directions.

There was no confusion over the direction or proximity of the source of the next sound however. It was very, VERY close. There was a sucking, popping noise behind them, like a strip of Velcro being pulled slowly apart. Then Whippet screamed.

Simon and Lucy spun round.

The scene before them was illuminated in all its horror. It wasn't a strip of Velcro being pulled slowly apart. It was the sound of eight giant tentacles sticking and un-sticking themselves to the surface of the bridge.

There was Whippet. No longer standing, but suspended in mid-air, upside down in the suckered grip of the largest of the blood-red tentacles that snaked up from beneath the bridge balustrade. The one that held him was scarred and cut. Here and there an arrow or a short-handled dagger protruded from its surface. The thing had clearly seen a lot of action. And it had survived.

'I HAAATE SQUIIID!!!' screamed Whippet honestly, as he was whipped backwards and forwards by the thrashing tentacle.

'Simon!' yelled Lucy. She reached behind her back and pulled out two items. The first was a home-made, handheld net-launcher. The second was a pair of earmuffs, which she promptly plopped on her head, before shouting to Simon, 'Give me a target!'

'Do what?' yelled Simon in surprise.

'Stop thinking for yourself and OBEY me,' shouted Lucy. 'The monster's moving too much! I need you to give . . . me . . . a . . . *target!*'

Simon felt the familiar rushing sensation as his power kicked into gear.

'You got it!' he replied, shutting his eyes. He breathed in. And out.

All those wriggling limbs. Moving like jelly. Hard to control. Perhaps he could slow it down. Yes.

He was a TELLER. So slow it down is what he did.

There was a fishing boat, long ago, called the *Salty Sue*. She housed a crew of two. Father and daughter, the Tackle family: Old Malt and Petal. Together they worked the boat through fair weather and foul. It was hard work and Old Malt had often tried to discourage Petal from joining him on his trips out to the deep and rough offshore waters, but Petal was having none of it.

She was a Tackle through and through, a superb sailor, sixteen years old, six foot tall and far stronger than Malt. He wasn't jealous of this last fact though, because he still had more tattoos.

And that's what really matters to a true sailor.

Yes, they were a legendary fishing partnership. It was rumoured the sea contained nothing they could not catch with the right bait, a strong line and plenty of tea and biscuits.

Rumours like that always lead to trouble, right?

And so it came to pass. One day, as they were making ready to take the *Sue* back out, a shadowy figure approached from the quayside with a unique offer. There was talk of a terrifying tentacled monstrosity terrorising boats in the shipping lane. The stranger offered a small fortune if the Tackles would capture such a beast. They accepted without hesitation. They'd seen some nasty sea critters and lived to tell the tale. But they should have stopped to consider that maybe, *maybe*, the worst was still out there. Lurking.

Moving . . . closer . . . closer . . . clossseeeeeerrr . . . and slowing down . . . slowing . . . slowing . . .

'PERFECT!' said Lucy, pulling the trigger on her invention.

Simon's story had frozen the beast in place, as he'd hoped it would. The wriggling limbs hung motionless. Lucy's contraption bucked violently in her grip and a huge net spat from the front of the device, expanding rapidly outwards. Small rockets attached to the edge of the net ignited, increasing its speed further. The net hit the tentacle with a wallop, just below Whippet, and wrapped itself around and around. It squeezed tighter and tighter until all of a sudden the tentacle quivered and its grip sprang open, releasing Whippet. The Thing dropped hurriedly out of sight.

'Yes!' cried Lucy in sheer delight.

'NO!' yelped Simon in horror, as gravity took hold of Whippet.

The Thing had been holding Whippet above the drop. He was no longer suspended over the bridge, and Simon could only watch as his best friend in all the world fell past him, eyes wide, mouth open, before disappearing without a sound.

'Whippet!' he yelled, running with Lucy towards the edge of the bridge. They peered over the side, down into the gloom, searching frantically.

'There,' shouted Simon, pointing.

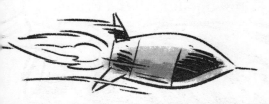

A pair of small eyes were staring back at them. Simon gasped. They weren't human.

'Gubbin? Is that *you*?!'

Lucy clenched her teeth and clambered over the edge of the bridge. 'Yes, that's my Gubbin! He's been keeping tabs on you two since you arrived, and I believe he just saved your best friend's life!'

It was true. Gubbin had somehow managed to catch Whippet by his socks before he fell to his doom like a poorly tossed pancake. The little cat-like creature was hanging by one long-fingered paw from a moose-head trophy mounted inexplicably to the outside of the bridge.

As if that wasn't impressive enough, in her mouth she held a sketchbook.

Working as a team they slowly hoisted both Whippet and Gubbin back up and onto the bridge where the group collapsed in an exhausted heap.

'I've said it before and I'll say it again,' panted Simon, 'life is never dull when you're around, Lucy!'

'And I've said it *twice* tonight, and I'm going to say it lots and LOTS more from now on until absolutely everyone I know truly understands how serious I am,' roared Whippet. 'I . . . *HATE* . . . squid!'

There was a pause, a cough and then the laughter exploded. It was loud and long and thoroughly deserved, the sort of side-aching chuckles that only come from a near-death experience at the tentacles of some rampant calamari.

CHAPTER 10

THE BIG (COMIC) PICTURE

All good laughing fits come to an end eventually. The children gathered themselves and their belongings, including Simon's Knuckles action figure, which he'd dropped during the Squid encounter. He still hoped to show it to Ernie at some point, although

the box was sadly looking a little battered from their recent scuffle.

Gubbin effortlessly jumped up onto Lucy's shoulder. Lucy beckoned the boys onwards.

'Er, what are we going to do about the octopus that's slithering about in your castle?' said Simon, with a backwards glance at the bridge.

Lucy gave Gubbin's head a gentle rub.

'Send it packing. But if we plan on beating that beastie, then we're going to need the right tools. And my supplies are THIS way. We're almost there.'

Lucy led them beneath first one, then a second miniature portcullis. Whippet and Simon stared up at the iron spikes of the gates hanging in a roof recess, high above their heads.

'Is that . . . rust on the spikes?' whispered Simon.

'Oh, please, please, *please* let that be rust,' moaned Whippet.

What sort of girl carries a net-launcher in their back pocket, just in case they run into a monster? I hear you ask. Indeed, what sort of girl lives in a private wing of a castle and has a bedroom barricaded behind a double set of lethal iron doors?

The world's bravest girl (uncontested) stopped before a plain door at the end of the corridor. She gripped the handle, twisted it and stepped inside. Simon and Whippet looked at each other. The portcullises made some sort of horrible 'Lucy' sense, but this last procedure seemed far too simple.

Lucy turned.

'What? Were you expecting some sort of intricate locking mechanism or deadly booby-trap device that needed to be disarmed, perhaps?' she asked.

The boys nodded enthusiastically. Lucy just smiled.

'Those gates back there are largely for show. Judging from your faces they had the right effect, but truthfully I don't need them. Any thief would have to be mental to break into *my* room. Now, let's get to work.'

At first glance, Lucy's room was a bit of an anticlimax. It was a normal shape and an average size. There was a bed sitting against the right-hand wall, beneath a window. Next to it stood a small wooden desk. There were a few shelves, each lined with books. And that was it.

'Huh,' said Simon in surprise. He couldn't help but feel a little disappointed.

Then he turned to check out something strange, off to his left, something his peripheral vision had initially imagined to be a poster or picture. Whippet followed him. The far wall of the room was covered with a spider's web. At least, that's how it appeared to Simon. As he drew closer he saw that the mass of lines suspended before them were in fact made from hundreds of pieces of red thread. It was spread across one entire wall. Behind the web was a giant map of Lake Shore, their town. Pins had been stuck into the map and the thread had been wound from one pin to the next.

'Pretty cool, isn't it?' said Lucy, sitting on her bed. Gubbin jumped from her shoulder and curled up on the duvet.

'I'd like to say yes,' said Simon, 'but I don't know what I'd be saying yes to.'

'What you see before you is the result of years and years of hard work. Every strange "happening" that has ever, er, happened in our little town has been recorded here. Over forty years of weirdness tagged and bagged.'

'You did all this?' said Simon.

Lucy tutted.

'How old do you think I am? Nope, I just continued what the Captain and T-Rex started. Well, I perfected it, actually. Those two have always been a little reluctant to get their hands dirty when it comes to smiting monsters.'

Simon's eyes widened. After their recent camping adventure Simon had been certain that Lucy and T-Rex knew each other . . . but Captain Armstrong too? It made a lot of sense. They were *all* monster hunters!

'Look,' said Lucy, jumping off her bed and crossing the room to flick a pin beside the Turnaway Bridge. '*Here* is where we found the lair of the Snotticus.'

She stretched up to point at another pin.

'And here was where the Screaming Haggle met its messy end.'

Simon and Whippet looked at the image of Wailing Wood. The events of their recent summer camp still gave them both nightmares.

'The threads show the order in which the events occurred and every pin is a monster that's been spotted, tracked or beaten. I've also pinned every crank sighting, hoax call or unproven claim from Joe and Judy Public.'

'Who?' said Whippet.

'The townsfolk. Every time some chump sees their own shadow and gets spooked they call the police to report a giant werewolf on the prowl or a bogeyman or something. We've been logging it, just in case it really *is* a bogeyman. This web is the end result.'

They stared in silence at the map.

'This is accurate?' asked Simon.

'To the millimetre.'

Simon squinted at the centre of the map.

His eyes widened. He pointed at the map and turned to Lucy.

'Well, if that's all true, do . . . do you think it's a coincidence that the building sitting right in the middle of this entire web is—'

'Castle Fearless? No. No, I don't.'

Lucy strolled to her desk where a pile of comics sat in a neat stack. Two dozen issues of **FREAKY** and **FEARLESS**.

'I said I thought the comics were connected, and they are. Each of these comics contains a monster that either we've encountered, I've fought on my own *or* that I've heard rumours about.'

She tossed a comic to Simon and another to Whippet.

'All the monsters out *there*,' said Lucy, 'have made their way into *here*.'

Simon flicked through the copy of **FREAKY**. There was Igor and the story of his electrical beast. It didn't make any sense.

Whippet shook his head in disbelief.

'That doesn't mean anything. Buster Brown must be using real-world monster sightings as inspiration for his drawings. I do that all the time with my own pictures.'

Lucy plucked the comic from Whippet's hand and whacked him round the head with it.

'Ow! Hey! What was that for?' moaned Whippet.

'I don't need a reason. Just haven't done it in a while,' said Lucy. '*But* if you need a reason, then ALL of these comics were published *too fast*. Sometimes they'd been printed BEFORE we'd even met the monster. This is all as fishy as a week-old trout wearing a winter coat on a warm day.'

Simon pointed to the centre of the map.

'Why isn't there a pin in the castle?' he asked.

Lucy looked at the wall. 'Well, nothing weird's ever happened here. And I should know.'

'HELLO?' hollered Whippet, jumping up and down and waving his hands like wobbly tentacles. 'SQUID! *SQUIIIIID!!!!*'

Lucy ground her teeth. She reluctantly picked out a pin from a small pot on her desk, crossed over to the map and stuck it into the castle.

'Okay, NOW something weird's happened,' she admitted reluctantly. She glared at the pin. 'That's really messed up my pattern.'

'Actually the Squid wasn't the weirdness I was thinking about,' said Simon.

He pointed to the bed. There, curled peacefully in a ball, was Gubbin. A strange little something if ever there was one.

'Where did he come from? What is he?' said Simon.

'Gubbin? I don't know. I think she's almost as old as me. Grandfather said she was a gift from a friend. Something to make me feel less lonely when I moved to the castle.'

Lucy fell silent. Gubbin looked from one child to the next and tilted her head to one side. She scratched her ear.

Slowly Lucy plucked another pin from the pot and buried it in the picture of Castle Fearless. She stood with her back to Simon and Whippet and slowly shook her head.

'I've been sloppy. I've missed details that have been staring me in the face and I've taken things for granted. We need answers, and that means finding Buster.

He's behind all this mess, and the madness ends tonight.'

She spun around, her face a picture of fiery determination.

'But before we face the final battle . . . do you want to see the REST of the place?'

CHAPTER 11

THE ERADICATOR

Lucy pressed a section of the wall opposite the door through which they'd entered. There was a click and a new, *hidden* door slid silently open before them.

A hum vibrated through the floor.

Simon stared through the doorway into a far larger room. The glowing screens of a dozen monitors sprang to life with beeps and bleeps. Lights hidden in wall and ceiling panels lit up, casting a soft glow around the room. Somewhere nearby a printer started chattering. A radio kicked into life, and a low-level hum of static filled the space. The white noise of the room waking up sur-rounded them. Simon found it strangely comforting.

The boys picked their way through stacked box files. They were heaving with piles of blurred photos, old yellowed case files and countless evidence bags. Simon stopped to pick up an item from a nearby pile. Inside the clear plastic bag was a piece of meat. It certainly looked like a piece of meat. A steak perhaps. Lucy's lunch?

Simon looked at the writing on the bag. It read: *Big Foot's Tongue?*

Simon dropped the bag, gagged and wiped his hands frantically on his trousers.

Unsurprisingly, the rest of Lucy's private wing contained a lot more than an ordinary bedroom with a small desk and a map covered in red thread and pins. Through the sliding door the boys discovered a training facility, complete with assault course, target range, martial-arts dojo, boxing ring and fully stocked gymnasium. Unable to believe their eyes, the boys traipsed across the space and through another set of doors, where they found themselves in an immense storeroom. Weapons, armour and

indescribable gadgets lined the walls, suspended from hooks and balanced on tidy racks. Lined up neatly on the floor, beneath a long shelf that was piled high with what looked like smoke bombs, were five identical versions of Lucy's remarkable backpack. The last time Simon had seen that bag it was flying through the air, having been knocked into space by a rampaging bird of prey.

Simon nudged Whippet. 'No wonder she wasn't bothered about losing her bag when we fought the Haggle!'

'Five more . . . wow . . . Mossy, this place is *crazy*. It's like some sort of mad villain's lair!'

'I thought about villainy, but it's not my style,' said Lucy, as she absentmindedly tossed a smoke grenade in the air and deftly caught it behind her back.

They moved on. A final archway led them to a vast workshop. Partially finished contraptions sat on workbenches, and tools lay scattered beside trays of screws and boxes of multicoloured wire and nuts and bolts and a whole lot of things that Simon didn't recognise.

Whippet walked up to a chalkboard that was propped against a cabinet. A childish drawing of a bazooka was scrawled in scratchy white upon the black.

'Hey, before you go all "Whippet" on me, don't judge my art, okay?' said Lucy defensively, grabbing a piece of chalk and scribbling over the picture on the board.

'I was just going to ask what it *was*, that's all,' said Whippet, staring at the mess of lines.

'Normal weapons don't work on these monsters, right?' said Lucy. 'I seem to be able to design and make stuff that slows them down a bit – like my net-launcher – but my inventions rarely work more than once. There's always some small flaw. When I sit in my workshop with Gubbin on my lap, I find I have all these amazing ideas, fantastical devices . . . but I can't get them out of my head and on to the paper.'

As if on cue, Gubbin padded softly across the room and curled himself around Whippet's legs. Simon saw it happen and felt the room pulse. He knew that sensation well. He knew what was coming. Whippet's power.

Was this the trigger? Coming into contact with something weird?

A course of energy shivered up Whippet's legs. His eyes grew wide.

'What . . . ? What do you . . . want it to *do*?' Whippet whispered.

Lucy tossed the chalk to Whippet, who caught it without even looking. His eyes stayed glued to the board. Lucy had noticed the change in him as well. She flicked her gaze down to Gubbin, who was lying, now seemingly asleep, on Whippet's feet.

'That picture is supposed to be my

"Eradicator". I built a sort of prototype once before, but I never got to use it. Don't even know if it would work. It just disappeared. It was a machine that could remove a monster's need to destroy things, get rid of its *desire* to cause trouble.'

'That's not very, well . . . "Lucy",' said Simon. 'Don't you prefer blowing things up?'

'Sure, but all-out destruction hasn't got me very far. I'm trying a new tactic. It still *looks* like a bazooka, and besides, the Eradicator doesn't *just* warp their minds.'

'What else does it do?' said Simon suspiciously.

'It blows them up.'

Simon had to laugh at that.

'Hey, I don't plan on changing *that* much,' said Lucy.

'The . . . *Eradicator* . . . *HOW does it work?*' said Whippet.

Lucy and Simon looked at their friend.

Whippet's hand was raised before the black-board, the chalk dangling from his fingers.

'Right, okay, so, I got the idea from an issue of **FEARLESS**. Knuckles used a similar device against some villain. It was a pistol originally, and it was supposed to emit a beam of energy – erasing energy – that worked a bit like the eraser on the end of a pencil. The beam could just sort of rub out the bad thoughts, the ones that caused all the problems. But I had no idea where to even begin . . . I'm a *fighter* not a scientist . . .'

'Well, I am a CREATOR...'said Whippet.

And so he drew.

And the chalk dust flew.

And he drew and he DREW.

Lucy whispered to Simon as they watched their friend work, 'Phone home and tell your parents that you're sleeping over.'

'Why?' said Simon.

'Because you're sleeping over,' said Lucy. 'The gap in time between the appearance of each new monster has been shrinking and shrinking, and my calculations point to a big KA-BOOM on the horizon.'

Simon took out his phone. He scrolled to his mum's mobile number. The phone rang and rang, then went to voicemail.

'Of course,' said Simon, 'she's at the cinema with your mum, Whippet. Her phone must be on silent.'

He quickly dialled his home number. There was a click from the other end of the phone.

'Hello!' came a small voice.

'Ruby?'

'No. It's Queen Bossypants.'

'Ruby, can you put Danica on?' said Simon.

Simon heard Ruby bellow her baby-sitter's name, and then she dropped the phone. There was a clunk, a pause, and then a rattle as the receiver was lifted.

'Are you in trouble?' asked a calm voice.

'How did you . . . ? Wait, Danica, we're not always in trouble, you know,' said Simon, a little too quickly.

There was silence from the other end. Simon pushed onwards.

'Whippet and I are, er, having a sleepover at the castle. With Lucy. Who lives here. So can you tell my mum not to worry and that everything's fine. Absolutely fine.'

'Put Whippet on the phone so I know he's okay,' said Danica.

Simon turned to look at his friend. He was scribbling away like a madman. So much chalk dust was flying up as he drew that Whippet had become coated in the stuff. He now resembled a ghost.

'Er . . . Whippet's a little . . . *distracted* . . . but he wanted you to know that he's fine. FINE.'

There was a small intake of breath.

'He actually *said* that?'

'Sorry, got to go! Bye,' gabbled Simon in a hurry.

He turned off his phone at the exact moment that Whippet's hand fell limply to his side. A tiny nub of chalk dropped from his fingers and rolled across the floor to rest against Gubbin's paw. Gubbin patted it away.

Lucy wafted a cloud of chalk dust from the air and approached the board. She knelt and studied the picture. It was unlike anything Whippet had drawn before.

'You boys and your powers. What I wouldn't do for a power of my own! I tell Whippet what to create and, look, he draws a schematic.'

'A what?' said Simon, staring at the drawing.

'A schematic. You know, a *plan*. A construction drawing. It's a set of instructions on how to build the Eradicator.

And it's . . . perfect . . .'

Lucy grabbed a sheet of paper and began to copy Whippet's drawing and instructions. Simon patted his friend on the shoulder.

'I didn't know you could do that, buddy,' said Simon.

'Neither . . . Neither did I . . .' said Whippet, panting, 'but Lucy has a very persuasive manner! I've a feeling I was given a push in the right direction too.'

The boys looked at Gubbin.

'Yep, I felt that too. Funny how our powers only seem to work when we're standing near something odd,' said Simon.

Before he could expand on his theory, however, a bell sounded. The same bell they'd heard before, booming up, rising from the deep, resonating and rebounding through the walls to shake the room and vibrate within their chests. But this time the peals rolled on and on. The noise surrounded them. Engulfed them. And then it was gone.

Lucy stood, folded her copy of the schematic in half and stuffed it in the pocket of her shorts. She raised her wrist and checked the time.

'The party is just about to start.'

'Are you talking about that bell?' said Whippet.

'Yep. That noise we just heard was the great peal of the Castle Fearless Clanger – the giant clock-tower bell. The giant *broken* clock-tower bell that has been ringing at random, off and on, for as long as I can remember.'

Lucy swung one of her fearsome backpacks on to her shoulder.

'But I'm starting to get the feeling that perhaps it hasn't been ringing randomly at *all*. Let's find out, shall we?'

CHAPTER 12

COUNTDOWN

Knuckles didn't hear the bell, but he felt it. The vibration of the peals. Bad news, getting worse by the minute.

Should he stay or go? Fight here, or flee to a different battle? Decisions, decisions . . .

It was all coming undone. He felt as torn as the PANEL hidden behind him. Torn between his sense of duty and his desire to help those he had left behind. He knew

Armstrong and T-Rex should be able to fix whatever mess was unfolding at home. But what if they couldn't . . . ? Out here, he was the last line of defence. He sighed and wrung the sweat from his mask. He would stay.

And far away, across the plain but getting closer, the tide swept on.

Hoofs. Claws. Paws. Limbs. Jaws. Two legs or four.

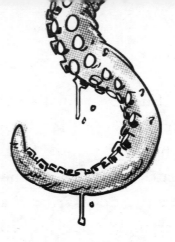

CHAPTER 13

BATTLE IN THE BELFRY?

The trio ran back through the castle. Gubbin had seemed content to stay safely in Lucy's quarters, almost as if he knew bad news was coming. Back in the armoury, Lucy had asked them to select a weapon of their own choosing. Faced with so many dangerous options, and so little time, Simon and Whippet had been unable to decide.

Frustrated, Lucy had hustled them out, muttering comments like, 'Boys are as useful as a chocolate teapot,' and, 'Couldn't operate a pair of trousers if they weren't shown where to find their legs,' and, 'Why is Simon carrying a Knuckles action figure into battle instead of a broadsword?'

As they'd passed along the first corridor, Lucy had dropped both portcullises behind them. Simon took this as a pretty bad sign. The boys had then been forced to run doggedly after the world's smallest adventurer, who set a tough pace. Simon soon found himself panting as they sprinted, climbed staircases three steps at a time, raced up ladders and at one point swung over a perilous gap, using Lucy's grappling hook.

Finally they drew to a halt at the bottom of a narrow spiral staircase that wound up the inside of a circular stone room.

'Okay, this is the bell tower,' said Lucy, craning her neck to study the structure or check for trouble, or both.

'*Puff* . . . Are . . . *pant* . . . Are we going up there?' wheezed Whippet.

'Yes,' said Lucy, 'but not without a plan of attack.'

'Oh, good,' said Whippet. He made the word *good* sound as if he meant the word *bad*.

'You think something's up there? What . . . like, the Squid?' said Simon.

Lucy snarled, 'Exactly. Look at the ooze on the steps. It's one thing for monsters and weirdos to terrorise the town of Lake Shore, but it is something else for them to invade *my* home!'

Invade. The word thundered through Simon's head, like a . . . stampede.

'It can't escape,' said Lucy, interrupting

his thoughts. 'This is the only way out. Whatever's up there is going to have to get past us.'

'Oh, goody,' said Whippet.

Escape. Again the word jangled in Simon's ears, but there was no time to think about that now.

Lucy grabbed Whippet by the jacket lapel and began to pull him up the stairs.

'Showtime!' she growled over her shoulder.

And so they climbed. Slowly, step by step, being careful not to make a sound, the trio tiptoed up the staircase. When they were halfway up, they heard a thump from above. Then a crash. Then a yell.

'Er, that came from . . .' began Simon.

'UP!' bellowed Lucy, and she charged at full speed towards the small doorway at the top of the tower.

Lucy combat-rolled into the room, and came up in a crouch, a torch in one hand and her familiar handheld crossbow in the other. She scanned the space, right to left. Simon and Whippet peered nervously round the door frame. They were slightly less keen to come face to face with a cornered monster.

But as it happened, for once they had nothing to fear. The room was empty.

'Glad you had my back,' said Lucy sarcastically.

'Hey, that's not fair. "UP!" is not a proper plan of attack,' said Simon as the boys joined her.

She shook her head and sniffed the air. 'Smell that?'

'Seaweed . . . fish . . .' said Simon. 'Definitely our guy.'

'But where did it go?' said Lucy. She moved over to the window and leaned out.

Whippet twitched. Something had dripped on his arm.

'I think you need to get your grand-father to fix the roof up here, Lucy,' said Whippet. 'It's leaking.'

Lucy paused in her search, then turned to face Whippet. She whispered 'It hasn't rained in weeks.'

Simon dry-swallowed and slowly looked up as Lucy shone her torch at the ceiling. Whippet's mouth fell open.

The Squid was curled around the inside of the bell tower . . . right above them!

'Oh my—' began Whippet, but his next words were extinguished.

There was a shout from behind them and a blinding light. They were forced to shut their eyes against the glare. Then there came a very moist-sounding explosion.

Whippet risked a peek and gagged. The ceiling was no longer occupied by the gigantic Squid. It was instead coated in thick, oozing purple gunk. And lots and lots of bits of *former* Squid.

As they watched, the remains of the monster decided to unpeel themselves from the roof and landed, with the wettest of *SHLUPS*, upon the helpless children.

Simon coughed and spluttered and

struggled his way out from beneath a large section of tentacle. The others were already getting to their feet. All three were coated in purple slop. Simon looked at the action figure still clutched in his hand. The box was completely ruined. He wiped his hands and pulled Knuckles free of his packaging. It was becoming increasingly unlikely this proof of their super-fan status would ever be shared.

Waste not, want not, thought Simon, and shoved the toy into the pocket of his trousers. It was a rare model after all.

'Bleugh! It's like the Snotticus all over again,' wailed Whippet.

'No, it's not,' said Lucy, 'because WE vanquished the Snotticus – remember?'

'However it happened, I'm pretty grateful,' said Simon, shrugging his way out of his filthy, sodden jacket.

Whippet raised both eyebrows so high that Simon feared the top of his head might pop off.

'Well, we don't have to battle it now, do we?' said Simon.

A smile spread across Whippet's face as he caught up with Simon's thinking. He

clapped his goopy hands together, laughed, and gazed up at the roof.

'Self-destructing Squid? No. Someone or something else did this, just before I could attack. But *who* or *what*?' said Lucy.

'Quick question,' said Whippet. 'Now . . . this is the BELL tower?'

'Obviously it's the bell tower, dummy,' said Lucy, waving her hand at the room in general.

'Right, only – and I don't want to add another mystery – it's just . . . well . . . where's the bell?'

Three faces gazed up into the purple-splattered belfry.

There was no bell to be seen.

CHAPTER 14

SHOTS IN THE DARK

'Change of plan – I'm calling for help,' said Simon, pulling his mobile phone from his pocket.

'No, we can fix this thing ourselves,' said Lucy.

Simon entered the number for the emergency services and pressed dial. He turned to Lucy.

'You might be right, and I know *you* are ready for anything, but in the past we've been lucky. Powers or no powers, there's something here, in the castle, that's more dangerous than a monster. A monster *destroyer* . . . a bell *eater* . . . and that scares me!'

'But *I'm* more dangerous than a monster,' said Lucy with a growl.

'Yes, and Simon and I are already scared of *you*,' said Whippet, dropping his slimy jacket on the floor.

The phone rang in Simon's ear. 'I just think we should let the professionals know about all this,' he said. 'Before it gets any worse.'

At that moment his phone decided to fly. It flew out of his hand and across the room, where it ended its flight pinned to the brickwork by an arrow. Simon looked from his empty hand to the wall. The arrow had drilled a hole right through his phone. It was useless . . .

The whole thing had happened so fast Simon didn't even think to jump out of his skin. Then reality caught up.

'L-Lucy?' he asked in a shaky voice. 'D-Did you j-just shoot my phone?'

Lucy vaulted over the remains of the Squid and ran to the back of the room. She reached up and yanked loose a long, thin object that was buried in the stonework. Then she spun on her heel.

'Arrow,' she yelled, 'but *I* didn't fire it! *Take cover!*

They ducked and frantically scampered on all fours towards the back of the room. A small table was propped against the wall, which Lucy kicked onto its side, to provide them with cover.

But there were no more arrows. After a few minutes hiding, during which nothing seemed to be happening and everyone got a bit bored, they slowly got to their feet.

'Someone or something shot my phone,' squeaked Simon.

'Someone or something blew up a squid,' whimpered Whippet.

'Someone or something just topped my TO-DO list,' snarled Lucy.

Under Lucy's direction, the trio searched the bell tower from top to bottom, but they found nothing useful. Based on the direction of the arrow, whatever had attacked them had fired from the doorway.

'They must have followed us up the stairs,' said Whippet.

'Or they were hiding in here when we entered, and snuck out while we were buried beneath that seafood platter,' said Lucy. She gave a lump of tentacle a kick for good measure. 'Either way, we need to look elsewhere. Let's head downstairs and check the exits.'

They moved back through the castle. Lucy's feet were operating on autopilot, her map of the familiar corridors logged somewhere deep in her subconscious. As she led the way, she studied Whippet's plan for the Eradicator. Whippet busied himself by trying to remove a bit of errant squid from his ear. Simon chewed on his lip.

'Lucy, can I ask you something?' said Simon nervously.

'Only if it's relevant to the mission,' came the reply from behind the schematic.

Simon rolled this around in his mind before making a decision.

'It isn't. But I was just wondering . . . What, er, what happened to your parents? You don't have to tell us if you don't want to; it's just you said you were given Gubbin when you came to the castle and I thought I should ask . . . in case no one ever did.'

Whippet stopped picking his ear.

Lucy folded the plan and tucked it back into her pocket.

Then she gave a small cough. 'I don't know how it happened.'

'Sorry?' said Simon.

'No one does. I was too young. Just a baby, really. It happened when we were visiting my grandfather. One minute my mum and dad were here, and the next they were gone. They just vanished.'

'That's . . . That's terrible . . . I'm really sorry, Lucy,' said Whippet gently.

Lucy shrugged. She shrugged a lot, but this one seemed to Simon to say rather a lot.

'Don't go feeling sorry for me. Ernie agreed to look after me from the very day it happened, and I've had an amazing childhood running around this castle. Ernie and me made a pretty good family. We had a lot of fun. Until recently.'

Simon was amazed. In his experience Lucy could be pretty negative. There was an anger inside her he was only just beginning to get to grips with, but she sounded

positive about her upbringing, even without her parents around. She really was a most surprising nine-year-old.

'In the last year Ernie's changed. He's been more interested in running his empire. We've drifted apart a bit, I suppose.'

They plodded on in silence for a spell. Lucy appeared to be lost in her thoughts.

'And you know, "*vanished*" does not have to mean gone for good,' said Lucy suddenly. 'They could still be out there, my parents. Somewhere . . .'

Simon nodded.

'Definitely,' said Whippet. 'I mean, Ruby vanished and we found her!'

Lucy frowned, then rolled her shoulders. 'Right, well, that marks the end of the interrogation. Shall we get back to business?'

They descended another staircase and arrived in the central hallway. There was a flurry of activity by the main entrance through which Simon and Whippet had first entered the castle, just a few hours before. Ernie Shufflebottom and his aged butler Jeffrey were hard at work, nailing boards across the doorway and stacking sandbags against the woodwork.

'Grandfather, what's happening? What are you doing?'

Ernie turned to face them.

'Some mad fool shot at me with an arrow,' said Ernie. 'The spineless fiend fled outside and that's where they're going to stay. I've a horrible feeling it was Buster! Jeffrey and I have been busy barricading every entrance.'

'Buster? Shooting arrows?' said Lucy.

'It would appear so. Honestly, I thought it was *you* for a moment, dear,' said Ernie.

'I know the feeling,' said Simon, for which he received a kick in the shins from Lucy, 'but that arrow destroyed my phone and I really need to call my mum.'

'Never fear, young Simon. I shall replace your phone first thing in the morning. With a better model. It's the least I can do,' said Ernie with a warm smile.

Whippet studied the door.

'So we're stuck inside,' said Whippet, to no one in particular.

'It's the best place for us all,' said Ernie. 'Considering what's happened, yes, this is where we should be. The relevant authorities have been informed of developments, and the problem will be taken care of.'

Simon tingled. The STORY was reaching out to him, almost as though it were tugging at his sleeves. Closer and closer it rose, like bubbles in a bath.

But the sensation passed.

'Thanks for offering to replace my phone, Mr Shufflebottom, and for trying to keep us safe,' said Simon.

Ernie looked at Simon and gave him a warm smile.

'Just promise me you three will return to Lucy's wing and stay out of harm's way.'

Ernie and Jeffrey drifted away down the corridor, presumably to board up another door.

Lucy stared at her grandfather's departing back and cracked the knuckles on her right hand.

'Buster . . . shooting arrows? He's a little odd, but he's been a ridiculously loyal friend to my grandfather. Bit like a stray dog. And he always used to draw me the most amazing birthday cards.'

Lucy cracked the knuckles on her left hand. She seemed to come to a decision.

'If he's finally flipped, I want to see it for myself.'

'Okay, so let's make ourselves useful. Let's find out who's ringing that bell. Who knows, it could be Buster,' said Simon.

Lucy nodded. 'I was never going to hide safely away. We need to help Grandfather by solving this thing ourselves.'

'Actually, we need to *find* the bell first,' said Whippet. 'When I last heard it, the bell

sounded like it was coming from under-ground.'

'Impossible. This castle was built on top of the original ruins. Grandfather said the foundations start at ground level. There's nothing beneath our feet but tonnes and tonnes of concrete,' said Lucy.

Simon shook his head. 'I've got to agree with Whippet,' he said. 'The sound I heard was pretty muffled but it was definitely rising up from beneath us.'

Like the STORY, he thought. *There is something buried here that someone doesn't want us to find.*

Lucy folded her arms. 'I've lived in Castle Fearless my whole life, explored every corner of every corridor, cubbyhole and cubicle. I would have found something.'

'But you weren't looking for a way *down*,' said Simon gently. 'You didn't think there was anything to find below ground level, so you didn't look.'

'Well, I'm looking *now*,' said Lucy, with a voice so icy it caused him to shiver.

And, as if sensing the need for additional drama, the missing bell began tolling once more.

CHAPTER 15

THE PANEL...
PART ONE

Knuckles was starting to think his decision all those years ago had been a terrible mistake.

He was not the hero that everyone made him out to be. Hundreds of stories had been told in the pages of **FEARLESS** about the exploits of the mysterious masked man and the search for his stolen identity, but none of them were true. Knuckles knew that the truth was very rarely as interesting as the action and adventure and daring last-gasp escapes that filled the pages of the most popular comics in the world.

But . . . every now and again it *was*.

The truth that Knuckles now faced was so epic, so monstrous, that it would blow the roof off the world. It was too much truth.

So he did what he could.

A number of beasts had reached the canyon and surged into the valley, arriving first alone, then in twos and threes. They were the head of the stampede. The fastest runners, flyers and crawlers.

Which was fine by Knuckles, because it meant he was yet to face the really heavy hitters.

Leaping from rock to rock, he vaulted into the procession and, one at a time, tackled each monster to the ground. He bound their feet with rope and moved on to the next without pause. He blindfolded

those creatures that had eyes, in order to calm them down. He had no intention of causing any additional distress. These were not the ones to fear. It was not their fault.

The Squids and the Haggles. *They* were the problems.

Now, lying before him, was a pile of quietly growling monsters. Subdued and bound. He had done well, but he had not caught them all. Another one had passed through the PANEL. That number would grow and grow until he was, finally, overwhelmed.

He thought of the boy. He thought of the girl. He thought of the woman who had known the danger of marrying a man who lived two lives.

He would struggle on.

For all of them.

And hope for a miracle.

CHAPTER 16

LUCY + BOMB = *BOOM!*

Simon, Whippet and Lucy entered the Library of WOW. They had attempted to trace the source of the clanging bell but had found it difficult to determine where it was coming from. The noise ricocheted off the walls in every direction. Then the bell had fallen silent.

Leaving them facing the library.

'Are . . . are we looking for a secret entrance to a hidden dungeon?' said Whippet.

'It would seem that way,' said Lucy.

'A secret entrance to a hidden dungeon that leads to a giant bell that's being rung by a person or persons unknown, probably for some really awful reason?' said Whippet.

'Uh-huh.'

'Good, good. Just wanted to be sure. Out of interest, how do you think other children are spending *their* summer holidays?' said Whippet in a panicked voice.

Simon thought back to Captain Armstrong's Shipshape Shop.

'I'm pretty sure they're still rioting,' he said. 'Which reminds me, where's Captain Armstrong? Do you think the Captain had barricaded himself inside his own shop? I guess I thought he might have been here to see us – after all, he did deliver the invitations.'

'*He* could be the one ringing the bell!' said Lucy. 'When he's not in his shop, he's almost always here, somewhere. I've seen more of Captain Armstrong than I've seen of Buster in the last few years. Either way, we won't know unless we find a way down.'

She dropped her rucksack and rummaged deep inside. First she pulled out a pair of night-vision goggles . . . and then a bomb.

'WHOA!' shouted Whippet, waving his arms. 'What are you doing?'

'Oldest trick in the book,' said Lucy.

'What books are *you* reading?' said Whippet, clutching at his hair in dismay.

'Relaaaaaax. Look, I put on the goggles, drop the bomb . . . and *bingo*.'

'Don't you mean *BOOM*-go?' asked Simon.

'It's not a real bomb, silly. It fills the room with an invisible dye, the sort they hide among bank notes to catch robbers. It'll only show up with my goggles. If there's a hidden door here, the dye will show us the way. It'll reveal every invisible crack and hinge.'

Lucy casually tossed the bomb into the middle of the room and tucked herself behind the door frame.

'It's not a traditional bomb but I'd still

hide if I was you,' she said. 'Invisible or not, the dye won't taste very nice, and it tends to get EVERYWHERE. And that's the point, really.'

Simon took the hint and hurled himself back through the entrance.

Whippet wasn't quick enough.

BOOOM!

When Simon re-entered the library, Whippet appeared to be trying to scrape his tongue off.

'Yuk! Gross! I can confirm, that stuff does not taste nice at ALL,' he whimpered.

Lucy ignored him. She was good at that. Now wearing her night-vision goggles, she turned slowly in a circle. Then she stopped, facing the part of the book-shelves that Simon and Whippet had destroyed earlier that day.

'Um, any damage you see was entirely accidental,' said Simon apologetically.

'That's not what I see,' said Lucy, and she passed Simon the goggles. He popped them on his head and was amazed. The library appeared to have been sprayed with a glowing blue paint. There, among the shelves, was a thin black rectangle.

Lucy felt around between the comics for a while, then nodded to herself. Simon heard a click and watched as Lucy pulled open a section of the shelving.

'Crafty old devil,' she muttered to herself, before grabbing her rucksack and heading through.

The doorway led directly into a metal lift. It was featureless except for one button that read: *BUSTER*.

Lucy muttered again and pressed the button. The door shut and the lift dropped. It dropped fast.

'Buster Brown? The **FEARLESS** artist?' said Whippet, holding on to one wall to steady himself.

'The very same.'

'Okay . . . but why work down *here*, underground?' said Simon. The lift was still descending, cranking and wobbling. They were deep, deep in the earth.

'I didn't know he did. He's always lived out of an office in Grandfather's wing of the castle . . .' said Lucy quietly. 'Seems I've been kept in the dark about a lot of things.'

The lift came to a stop.

The doors opened.

The children stepped out of the dark and into the light.

And once again their whole world was flipped on its head.

CHAPTER 17

THE PANEL...
PART TWO

It was a dungeon in the true sense of the word. There were cells. Lots of cells. Cells that stretched away into the gloom.

And almost every cell was occupied by a monster.

The children looked at each other but no one could think of anything funny or clever to say. Instead they simply crept quietly forward.

On either side of them, locked behind bars or floating in liquid-filled tanks, was a rather terrifying collection of creatures. Large, dinky, skinny, rotund, fiery, sticky, flying, multiple-limbed, eyeless, hairy, thorn-covered . . . the descriptions rolled on and on and on, for no two monsters were alike.

Simon and Whippet were exchanging hurried glances as they took in the contents of each cell.

'That's the Briney Bamboozler!' said Whippet in amazement.

'And . . . And this one, unless I'm mistaken, is Gutripper Snork. Had his own pull-out poster in **FREAKY** issue 2149,' said Simon.

He twisted his head left and right.

'Lucy? How is this possible? These are ALL creatures that have appeared in either **FREAKY** or **FEARLESS**!' whispered Simon.

'They're monsters from the comics,' said Lucy, as if she were still taking in the idea.

'Yes . . . but why are they so quiet?'

Apart from general background noise

of snuffles and scrapes as the monsters moved around in their cells, the dungeon was largely silent.

Lucy peered into the nearest cage. An ape-like beast sat with its head bowed. It flicked a quick glance at Lucy, then returned to staring at its huge ten-clawed paws. It didn't look all that terrifying up close. In fact . . .

'They look scared,' said Simon.

'Of what?' said Whippet in amazement.

The great bell rang out, filling the cavernous space. In unison, every monster turned in silence to stare at the other end of the hall.

'Let's find out,' said Lucy, and the trio crept forward once again.

The row of cells came to an end, and they approached a wide balcony. Simon risked a peek over the edge. His eyes grew wide. The scene playing out below him could have been stolen from the pages of Whippet's favourite comic . . . but it would have been a very strange issue, even for **FREAKY**!

The balcony was suspended above a wide stone amphitheatre that was illuminated by hundreds of fat candles stuck to the floor in clumps, like flickering bunches of flowers. An angled drawing board, similar to Whippet's own desk in his bedroom, was set up at the foot of the stone steps. It was surrounded by piles of comics, mountains of blank paper, bottles of ink, pencils, pens, rulers – basically all the apparatus needed to make the greatest comics on the planet.

To the left of the desk, a hunchbacked elderly man in an ink-stained blazer was frantically banging a giant bell with a beater. The bell from the tower! The man was so short that he was having to jump up and

down in order to reach it, which was a difficult manoeuvre as he was chained to the drawing-board desk by his ankle.

To the right of the desk was a pneumatic crane, with an extending arm. An empty cage was attached to the end of the arm.

In the middle of the space, Captain Armstrong and T-Rex were wrestling a bear. Well, it might have been a bear, if bears were yellow and had dragon tails and three heads. The Captain had the bear-thing's middle head in a headlock, and the other two heads were desperately trying to bite T-Rex. There was already a chunk missing from the Captain's wooden leg. It was rather hard to say precisely *who* was winning.

Yet while this was all fantastical stuff, the element that truly blew the minds of Simon, Whippet and Lucy stood at the back of the room. It was six metres high and three metres wide. A perfect white rectangle. It was outlined by a thick stroke of black. It could almost have been a cinema screen if it wasn't for the white. It was the kind of white that most white could only dream of becoming. It glowed. It positively pulsed. And it seemed to *call* to the children.

It said: I am the **PANEL**.

And the bear-monster-thing that Armstrong and T-Rex were battling was coming OUT of the strange white shape.

Simon gulped.

THIS was the story. This was the truth that had been tickling at Simon for weeks now.

'The monsters . . . have been coming from my basement?' snarled Lucy in disbelief. 'The monsters have been coming from *MY basement*!'

She sprinted towards a staircase that led

down towards the main room. Simon and Whippet followed as she descended to the amphitheatre steps and began to jump from one to the next, heading *towards* the chaos.

'Er, what are we doing?! How are we going to help?' yelled Whippet.

As it happened their assistance wasn't needed. Captain Armstrong swung his weight forwards, gave a huge heave, and in

a judo-style move he pulled the bear out of the glowing square and threw it over his shoulder. T-Rex grabbed it in mid-air and twisted sideways, hurling it into the empty cage, which promptly snapped shut. All three bear heads roared once in anger, then fell quiet. The fight was over.

Simon and Lucy ran to greet their friends. Whippet slowed to a walk. He stopped and turned to stare at the old man standing by the desk.

'Simon! Whippet! Lucy! How did you find this place? It be too dangerous,' said the Captain.

Lucy put her hands on her hips. Her face was all pinched up, tight with fury.

'We've survived worse, Captain! Now talk fast, because from where I'm standing it looks like you two are responsible for *all* our troubles!'

The Captain opened and shut his mouth a few times but no words came out.

'Lucy not blame Captain,' said T-Rex. 'Him try do right thing. Me try do right thing.'

Lucy spun to face the caveman. 'And what "right thing" was that?' she snapped.

T-Rex puffed out his cheeks. The Captain's shoulders slumped and he sat down heavily on the lowest step.

'It . . . It be . . . complicated, lass . . .'

said the Captain, with genuine sadness in his voice.

Simon sat down beside him. 'Start with something easy. Why is that big bell down *here*? Why have you been ringing it all night?'

'Aar, that be a simple one. We needed an early warnin' system, somethin' that could be 'eard from town. In case one of the monsters slipped past before we could restrain it. We've, er, been ringin' it a *lot* lately . . .'

'Oh, you've got a monster loose all right,' said Lucy, 'and she's *nine years old*!'

Whippet decided to leave Lucy to her heated interrogation. He shifted his attention to the old man, who had dropped his bell beater and returned to his desk. He was busy drawing, frantically scribbling, the tip of his tongue poking out at the side of his mouth.

Whippet swallowed. He'd never met a living legend before.

'Um . . . hello . . . I'm Whippet Willow. I'm your number-one fan,' he said, holding out his hand.

The man nodded and gave Whippet's hand a quick shake without even putting down his pen. He smiled.

'Buster Brown. Look at us two, eh?

Alliteration! W.W. and B.B. Two peas in a pod. Not to mention the fact we're both scribblers,' he said.

Whippet's eyes widened.

'You . . . you know I d-draw?' he stuttered in surprise.

'Of course I do! I judge all the art competitions in the comics. You, lad, are the REAL DEAL!'

Whippet bashfully kicked one foot against the other, then noticed his dishevelled appearance.

'I'm not normally this scruffy, Mr Brown, but I had a slight run in with some . . . er . . . purple stuff,' said Whippet, staring, embarrassed, at his stained T-shirt and hands.

'I'm one to talk, my boy. There are ink spots on this blazer that date back to 1969!'

Whippet gazed at the pictures emerging

from Buster's pen. It looked like he was drawing the glowing PANEL from the back of the room. But there was something dark about it. Something ominous. The panel Buster was drawing appeared to be standing on a pathway near a spooky forest.

'Did you really draw ALL those comics? **FREAKY** and **FEARLESS**? Every issue . . . all on your own?' he whispered.

Buster's smile faded. 'Unfortunately so, yes.'

'Amazing,' said Whippet breathlessly. 'I'd give anything to have your imagination!'

Buster placed his pen carefully on the drawing board and slowly extended his leg until the chain pulled taut.

'Be *very* careful what you wish for, Mr Willow,' said Buster. 'You might get more than you bargained for.'

'Er, why . . . ? Why are you chained up?'

whispered Whippet in horror.

'Because I tried to leave. I refused to make another comic. I've had enough, see? I just wanted to make the world a more exciting place for kids, give them stories and art to love. I don't want to be a part of this dangerous mess. It has to end. *This* will be my final comic ever. I have to *break the chain*!' He returned to his frantic scribbling.

Whippet slowly backed away from the desk. 'Guys . . . guys! Buster's been chained up over here! I don't know why, but he says he's trying to break free!' he hissed.

Four pairs of eyes turned towards Buster, but the artist never even raised his head from his work. He was completely engrossed and seemed unwilling or unprepared to speak further.

One individual, however, had something to say.

'Still planning on leaving the comics are you, Buster? That's a shame. Almost as foolish as our young guests discovering my dungeon,' said Ernie Shufflebottom.

The children spun on their heels. Lucy's grandfather was standing behind them.

'I did warn you not to explore the castle. This is extremely . . . *unfortunate*,' said Ernie with a deep sigh.

CHAPTER 18

A BRAVE NEW WORLD

Ernie swept across the room towards the cage. He stared for a minute at the bear-monster, then turned and gave Buster a sharp look.

'The bell?'

'We lost another,' said Buster pathetically. 'Been ringing it for ages. Not that it matters any more . . .'

'We'll discuss your "retirement" later,' said Ernie, 'but don't you have a couple of VERY late issues to draw? You're going nowhere until the job is done.'

Buster scowled and returned to his scribbling.

'Never missed an issue in my life, and this is my thanks . . .' he mumbled to himself.

Captain Armstrong stood up. 'We've been doin' our best, but there's barely been time to cage 'em all, let alone release the older ones back into the **PANEL**. A slippery squiddy thing managed to slip past us.'

Simon exchanged a glance with Lucy.

'I took care of that problem. Permanently,' said Ernie, staring at the three children in turn. 'You children don't have to thank me, but I was trying to save your lives.'

Lucy kicked the cage containing the bear-like beast.

'Grandfather, what have you done?' she asked with seething anger. 'There are monsters on the loose and monsters in cages and a great big glowing white hole in space in a basement I never knew existed! Have you been . . . bringing comic creatures to *life*?'

Ernie ground his teeth, then turned to face Captain Armstrong and T-Rex.

'Guardians, your services are no longer needed. I do not believe your dear friend's claim that there is a stampeding monster horde heading our way. He's been out in the wild too long. We'll be back to business as usual soon enough, and in the meantime you'd better return to your precious shop before the mob burns it down. I will look after the children.'

Armstrong and T-Rex gave a wary salute, then turned and headed towards the lift.

Buster watched them go.

'Ernie, that stampede — don't you think—' he began.

'I do. All the time. But you shouldn't. You're not here to think, you're here to draw,' said Ernie. 'So for the last time, will you just *DRAW*?!'

Ernie walked towards the **PANEL** and the children followed. Up close, the **PANEL** really was something to behold. It vibrated with possibility. Strangest of all, in

Simon's opinion at least, was the fact that it seemed to smell of newsprint.

Ernie stared at the whiteness. His pupils contracted against the light.

'Many a bad situation has arisen from a good intention,' said Ernie.

'What is that supposed to mean?' said Lucy.

'All we ever wanted was to bring joy to the lives of children everywhere.

That, and give you a childhood worth remembering,' said Ernie. 'And you know what, Lucy? You've been an angel these past few years.'

'No one's ever called me *that* before,' she muttered.

'Yes, well, it's true. I've been extremely careful down here, but even with the assistance of Captain Armstrong and T-Rex, certain . . . things . . . have escaped us.'

Simon stepped closer to the **PANEL**. It was drawing him in. Drawing them all closer to it.

'By "things", you mean the Snotticus and the Screaming Haggle?' he asked.

Whippet joined his friend. 'Simon's sister was kidnapped by one of those monsters!'

Ernie glanced at them and took a step backwards. Simon, Whippet and Lucy continued to stare at the **PANEL**. It was truly mesmerising.

'It used to be easy. T-Rex and the Captain caught a monster and brought it through, then we caged it and used it for

comic inspiration. I would write the beast into a storyline and Buster would draw it, in perfect detail. When we'd finished we released them back into the **PANEL**. No harm done.'

Ernie looked from one child to the next.

'They must have sensed the window into our world, because around eleven years ago they started to find their own way through. A few at first, but pretty soon we had too many monsters on our hands. They found cracks in the castle foundations. They dug holes. A few even worked out how to operate the lift. In short, they got out.'

Ernie took another small step. No one noticed.

'And while I've been unimaginably grateful for all Lucy's efforts in keeping the town of Lake Shore safe, you boys have achieved the supposedly unachievable and found my *rabbit hole*. I don't mind the world knowing that I print both **FREAKY** and **FEARLESS**. I don't even mind the world knowing that both comics have been written and drawn solely by Buster and myself . . .'

He took a sideways step behind the children, who were still staring in amazement at the **PANEL**.

'What I do mind, what I *cannot* abide, is anyone discovering the source of our inspiration! All the remarkable monsters and oddballs that have filled the pages of our comics, they're our trademark genius. No one can know that they're real! No, no . . . the **PANEL**, and everything that's ever stepped through it, must remain a secret forever.'

Another step.

'As I said before . . . this really is *most* unfortunate,' said Ernie.

And with that he gave Simon and Whippet a shove, straight into the **PANEL**.

There was a sound like paper being torn, and they disappeared.

Lucy's mouth dropped open. 'What . . . ? What did you just do?!' she shouted in disbelief.

'Protected your inheritance, my dear. A few rampaging monsters here and there and a couple of missing boys are a small price to pay for the continued happiness of children the world over, are they not? *The show must go on!* Besides, you don't even like boys . . . you don't *trust* them.'

Lucy swung back her leg and kicked Ernie in the shin with all her might, causing him to yelp in pain and hop up and down like a human pogo stick.

'Actually, I trust those two with my LIFE! And I'll prove it,' she snarled through clenched teeth.

And before Ernie could stop her, the world's smallest adventurer dived head first into the **PANEL**.

CHAPTER 19

THE *PANEL* . . .
PART *THREE*

Simon opened his eyes but it didn't help. His vision was clouded. His eyes were sore in a way that was hard to describe. He rubbed them and suddenly the colours rushed in, rolling over him like an explosion of water from a broken dam. Colour and colour and colour and colour and . . .

Oh my word, thought Simon.

The only way Simon could describe it to himself later was that it was like seeing in colour for the very first time. The reds were redder than a firework explosion. The greens lusher than a spring meadow. The blues were deeper than the sea and wider than the sky. It was hard to take it all in.

He tried to speak, but his mouth was as dry as sandpaper. Much like his eyes, it felt like he'd never used it before. He raised his hand and rubbed his lips.

GET UP! GET UP! IF YOU WANT TO LIVE, GET UP NOW!

bellowed Lucy. Her words hung in the air over their heads, literally, in a speech bubble. A second later they faded away.

Simon and Whippet didn't need to be told again. They jumped to their feet and tried to locate the source of their impending troubles. The boys found that they were standing in a bright valley. Strange plants and trees filled the wide space. It would have been a beautiful spot if not for the dozen monsters that were charging headlong towards them.

> HOOFS. CLAWS. PAWS. LIMBS. JAWS. TWO LEGS OR FOUR.

'Yep, that about sums it up, Mossy,' wailed Whippet miserably, and his words hovered before fading.

Simon had been thinking aloud again, but this time the words had felt different. They weren't just part of a story. It wasn't

just his special power booting up. It was almost as if he was reading someone else's thoughts. Someone close by . . .

'Where can we hide?' said Whippet.

The walls of the valley were too steep to climb, there was no cover within reach, and the **PANEL** was nowhere to be seen.

'We can't,' wailed Simon, instantly panicking that his word bubble would give them away.

'We don't need to,' said Lucy. 'We have one another. You have your powers. So, follow my lead, together!'

Whippet pulled his sketchbook from his pocket. The monsters were bearing down on them fast. The gap was closing and closing.

'I will show these monsters the true **POWER** of a Shufflebottom,' said Lucy, bunching her fists.

'We're with you till the end,' said Simon, clearing his mind.

The monsters roared on, although they didn't seem to be getting much closer, which Simon thought was pretty strange. Useful though, as it meant they had time to prepare.

Lucy felt an energy vibrate through her. Simon and Whippet felt it too. If Simon was the TELLER and Whippet was the CREATOR . . . then the world's smallest action heroine was the BOSS. And if there's one thing a BOSS knows how to do, it's give orders.

Lucy shouted:

BOOMERANG HARPOON!

Whippet drew on command. Lucy frowned.

Lucy shouted, 'BIGGER!'

Whippet drew on command. It was much bigger. Lucy shook her head.

Lucy shouted, 'MORE DARTS!'

Whippet drew the most ridiculous harpoon ever devised, complete with fifteen darts, and it ripped into existence.

Lucy grabbed it from him and took aim. 'We're going to need the TALLEST of TALES today, Simon,' she yelled. 'You've got to bring them *to their knees*!'

Simon opened his mouth. He closed it. He thought back to their battle with the Squid. He had wanted to turn the tentacles to stone but he had only been able to slow the monster. A nice idea but it wouldn't work here. There were too many beasts. He couldn't hypnotise them all.

But perhaps he didn't need to. They still didn't seem to be getting much closer. Was it an optical illusion? Either way, it gave him the time and space he needed.

Simon cleared his mind and began to tell a different sort of story: the *shortest* of tales. No set up, no characters. Simon spoke directly to the front row of monsters, who were now only thirty metres away. He told them that all their lives they'd been unaware that their legs were actually made of jelly. The monsters had never been spoken to like this before. They listened intently. They believed every word that flowed from Simon's mouth and into their ears. In their minds their legs were suddenly transformed to a sugary, wobbly dessert.

And *no one* can run when they've got pudding for legs.

The front row fell to the ground in a sliding heap, and rolled onwards, tumbling, rumbling, as the charging monsters behind them tripped over them and fell, adding to the pile-up. But the massed speed of the

horde still threatened to crush the children where they stood.

Then Lucy fired the harpoon. The rope tethers attached to the back of the fifteen boomerang darts arced outwards in a huge circle as they flew around the monster bundle before returning to where they had started, snaring them all in a giant lasso. The darts buried themselves deep in the dirt like javelins.

The lines snapped tight.

The bound mob of beasts was yanked to a violent stop millimetres from the feet of Simon, Lucy and Whippet.

'And *that* is how you get the job done,' said Lucy in delight, turning to the boys with a huge grin on her face. The harpoon was resting casually on her shoulder. She was every bit a comic-book warrior.

'All this time I've been secretly more than a little jealous that you boys have inherited such crazy powers. But look what I did! I think the power to BOSS BOYS AROUND TILL THEY DO WHAT I WANT is pretty priceless.' She laughed, her words shimmering as they dissolved.

'We might need your special skills again, Lucy,' said Whippet, pointing over her shoulder.

They all turned and stared up the valley.

A lone figure was approaching at a run. It was a man. As he drew nearer he slowed to a jog. He was wearing a long ripped and battered coat and his face was covered by a mask. Simon and Whippet gasped in unison.

Simon took a step forward. His hand fumbled for his pocket.

'It's . . . It's *KNUCKLES*!' said Simon breathlessly.

And it was.

Knuckles stopped beside the monster horde. He studied their writhing bodies. Simon's powerful words seemed to be having a longer-lasting effect here, for none of the monsters could stand up. They still believed they had jelly legs!

Knuckles shook his head.

'Is it really you?' asked Simon, stepping closer. '*How* can it be you? It's impossible. You're a comic character.'

'What YOU just performed should be impossible, but I saw it happen with my own eyes,' said Knuckles, 'and I heard your words. I heard you convince this mob that they had jelly legs. It seems to me, Simon Moss, that all your tall tales are finally coming true.'

Simon froze. He recognised that voice.

Knuckles reached up and grabbed his mask with both hands. He pulled it free and dropped it to the ground. Simon's and Whippet's mouths fell open. Lucy looked from one boy to the other.

'Do you know this guy?' said Lucy.

'You could say that,' whispered Simon, his pounding heart threatening to burst through his chest. 'He's my father.'

CHAPTER 20

SOME KIND OF FAMILY REUNION

Simon's dad fell to his knees, grabbed his son and pulled him into the biggest hug of his life. When they finally broke apart, both had tears in their eyes, but they were laughing.

HOW DID YOU ALL--

HAVE YOU BEEN--

WHERE HAVE YOU--

WHAT IS WITH THE--

Their word balloons overlapped and popped against each other and they stopped interrupting each other and laughed again. Simon's dad held up his hand.

'Me first. Actually, because we don't have much time, me *only* for now.'

He took a deep breath.

'It's true that I am Knuckles, but I am not a comic hero. I have no powers, not like you boys. Long, long ago – long before you were born, Simon – when I was a little boy, I found the **PANEL**. I'd been playing in the old dungeon ruins of the castle, back before Ernie bought the land and built the new Castle Fearless. I saw it all happen. I watched T-Rex literally *tear* his way into our world.'

'Our T-Rex?' said Lucy.

'The very same. Now he *is* a comic character, in the real sense of the word. You are standing in his world. T-Rex told me it was just an accident. He was messing around, testing his strength and he simply tore a hole through from his world to ours. It's not that hard to believe when you realise this is a COMIC world. The walls between dimensions are only paper thin. You've seen the **PANEL**, right? Pure comic.'

Simon felt in his pocket. He pulled out the Knuckles action figure and gazed from

the painted plastic face in his hand to his father.

'You . . . You said you worked for the government . . . but you're *Knuckles*?' said Simon.

His dad cast his eyes downwards.

'That job was a cover story. I work for Lucy's grandfather. Always have. I kept the truth from you because I wasn't sure you were ready for it. I was wrong. As a boy, like you, I wanted to know *everything*, all the time. And more than anything I wanted to know where T-Rex came from. You see, we became friends on that day. I became his guide to Earth, and he was mine here, in the land of Comic.'

He picked up his mask and stood up.

'We agreed to keep each other's true identities a secret. Here in Comic, being "normal" makes you stand out from the crowd. Everyone here is a bit of an oddball, especially the monsters. So I invented Knuckles. He was a great character to make-believe. A brave hero searching for the truth, whose true identity had been stolen. It wasn't all that far from my own story.'

'Grandfather *found* the **PANEL** in the basement, didn't he?' asked Lucy. 'When he bought the old castle ruins?'

'He did,' said Simon's dad, 'but more importantly, he stumbled upon me and T-Rex climbing back through the **PANEL**. I was still in my costume so he believed I was another character. Another alien.'

He waved at the valley around them.

'Ernie was a different man back then. He wanted to keep the **PANEL** a secret in order to protect this incredible place from those on Earth who might want to take advantage.'

Simon thought about the cages. 'But

that's not what happened,' he said sadly.

His father shook his head. He raised the sleeve of his jacket and checked his watch.

'We don't have long. Listen – Ernie and Buster, they only wanted to help. They built their headquarters and locked the gates and allowed no one in and effectively hid the **PANEL** from prying eyes. All they asked for in return was a little . . . inspiration. For a pair of comic creators they've never been big on original ideas. But they tell good stories.'

'Inspiration. You mean, the *monsters*,' said Whippet.

'Yes. Ernie had a noble aim. He wanted to entertain the children of the world with the greatest comics ever created. I was a kid at the time. I saw what they built and I loved it. There was no need for cages back then.

We only brought one monster through at a time for them to work from, and T-Rex and I were able to keep the creatures calm before returning them to Comic. Captain Armstrong joined us after a while, and together the three of us worked for Ernie, protecting the bridge between the worlds while keeping them supplied with ideas for the comics, **FREAKY** and **FEARLESS**.'

Simon slapped himself on the forehead. 'Captain Armstrong knows where I live because he knows I'm your son . . . right?'

'Yes. He and T-Rex have always tried to keep an eye on you when I've been away.'

'What changed?' said Lucy. 'What did my grandfather do?'

Simon's dad rubbed his chin. 'Ernie kept wanting to increase the thrills. He needed more dangerous material and, foolishly, we agreed to bring some less *harmless* monsters through the **PANEL**. That was our big mistake. Ernie's appetite for trouble has been almost as endless as yours, Lucy.'

'No, he's worse,' said Lucy in a small voice, her eyes shining. 'He pushed the boys through the **PANEL**.'

'He did what?' said Simon's dad. He sounded horrified.

'He's desperate. Running out of ideas,'

said Lucy. 'He invited Simon to Castle Fearless as a prize for a short-story competition he didn't even win, because he thought we were on to him. Then he boarded up the castle, to keep a closer eye on us. I think he shot an arrow through Simon's phone to stop us calling for help. It seems he'd do anything to keep the **PANEL** secret.'

Simon's dad blinked. 'He really pushed you both through?' he said.

Simon shrugged.

Whippet frowned.

Lucy nodded.

'He saved us earlier . . . but yeah . . .' she said.

Simon's dad stood stock still. Then he pulled his mask back on. Only his eyes were visible but they no longer belonged to Simon's dad. They were the eyes of Knuckles, and they were burning with fury.

'FIRST we're going to stop this stampede,' he growled, 'and then we're going to have a little "chat" with Shufflebottom senior.'

CHAPTER 21

THE INCREDIBLE MONSTER-STOPPING MACHINE

They stood at the entrance to the canyon and watched in silence. No one needed binoculars. The stampede was close enough to smell.

'Dad, in my short story, I . . . I wrote

about this,' said Simon.

'Yes,' said Knuckles, 'I've long suspected you had a *real* connection to Comic, but I never knew Whippet possessed a power. A TELLER and a CREATOR. With Lucy as your BOSS? An unstoppable trio. T-Rex told me there used to be others like you three, once upon a time.'

'But how did we get these powers? From fighting the monsters?' asked Simon.

'If it was *that* easy I'd be the most superpowered dad in the universe,' said Knuckles with a short bark of a laugh. 'I think you were just born with them. Your encounters with the inhabitants of Comic – Captain Armstrong, T-Rex, Gubbin and, yes, the monsters – have brought them to the surface, but that's all. You've either got them or you haven't, and clearly you have.'

Simon swallowed.

'Dad, I can do things . . . change things. Did my story *start* this stampede?'

'No, this is the inevitable end of a conga line that we started. T-Rex tore a hole in the world and then we showed the monsters the way through. And guess what? They talked to each other. We thought when we returned them to Comic they'd just go back to their own lives, but this world is crazily dangerous. There are things here that *terrify* the average monstes. So, would *you* rather be a predator in a land full of predators, or a predator in a world filled with soft human-shaped prey?'

No one said anything for a while. They knew the answer.

'We have to find a way to stop them. If that lot reach the **PANEL**, they will overrun the castle, destroy the town and there'll be no way to turn back the tide,' said Knuckles.

Lucy coughed. They all turned to face her. She was waving a sheet of paper in her hand.

Whippet squinted. 'Is that my schematic?' he said.

'For the Eradicator, yes. This is the key,' said Lucy.

Knuckles took the drawing from Lucy and studied it carefully.

'Some of these parts look familiar,' he said. 'I used something like this to fight Dr Danger in issue 1845 of **FEARLESS**, although mine didn't look like a bazooka.'

He looked up at Lucy. There was sadness in his eyes.

'You know who came up with the idea for my original Eradicator?'

Lucy shook her head.

'Your mother,' said Knuckles.

Three mouths dropped open in surprise, but Knuckles didn't give them a second to react.

'Hmm. Two problems spring to mind. Firstly, this is a mind-control device. It might work on a few monsters at a time, but not that mob. Their will is too strong.'

'I agree,' said Lucy, 'but ... wait ... My mother?'

'No time for questions. Not now. The second problem is that, if I remember correctly, this device has a *very* unstable power core . . . It would probably explode the first time you turned it on, and erase anything in its path.'

Lucy nodded. 'I agree,' she said again, a small smile playing on her lips.

'I'm not going to destroy any monsters,' said Knuckles. 'That's not how I work.'

Lucy continued to smile. Simon was the first to catch on.

'No, Lucy is suggesting we use the Eradicator on the **PANEL**, not on the monsters. She wants to rub it out. To permanently stop them finding a way through,' said Simon.

'But that would mean we'd be stuck here. Forever,' said Whippet in horror.

Knuckles looked at Lucy, then pointed to the plans. 'Can you actually build this?'

'Yes,' said Lucy, 'if I had the right tools and materials.'

Knuckles pulled a small device from his pocket. It wasn't quite a phone, it wasn't quite a video-game controller. But it was very, very Comic. He hit a button and the children heard a voice bark from the speaker.

'What's up, boss?' said the voice.

'Duster, head to Tin Can's scrapyard and fill the *Silent Kite* with all the salvage she can carry. The weirder the better. I need it *now*. Come down on these coordinates.'

'One last-minute rescue coming up, boss! See you in a second,' replied Duster from the communicator. And he was true to his word.

Mere moments later, an MV-22 Osprey Seaplane soared into the valley and came to a graceful landing beside the group. The pilot jumped down from the cockpit to greet them.

'It's Duster . . . from the comic,' said

Simon, to Whippet's amazement. 'Duster from *Knuckles and Duster*!'

'The very same! Boss, you wanted scrap, I got you scrap, but I'm not hanging about. There's a stampede on the way, if you hadn't noticed,' said Duster, then he thumped a button on the side of the plane.

The rear loading bay door opened and onto the grass poured more odds and ends and tools and junk than seemed possible to fit into the vehicle. Lucy dived in and started selecting what she needed.

Then she turned and ordered Whippet to join her, in *that* tone of voice.

Simon watched in amazement as his friend obediently ran over and began to sort and stack components.

'Oh, I love my power,' said Lucy gleefully.

'Get going, Duster. And in case I

don't get the chance later, thanks. For everything . . .' said Knuckles.

Duster climbed back into the cockpit. He threw a sharp salute to Knuckles, taxied the plane in a tight circle and took off.

Simon watched him fly clear of the valley.

'Are you absolutely, one hundred per cent, totally sure you're not *really* a comic-book hero?' whispered Simon.

Knuckles grinned and ruffled his son's hair.

'Okay, it's done,' said Lucy from behind them.

The machine that stood on the grass was . . . original. It seemed to have changed rather significantly from the original drawing, and this was largely because of the materials available. Duster's scrap had held all the necessary components, but the scale

had shifted slightly. The machine looked less like a bazooka, more like a cross between a giant hairdryer and a tractor.

Simon stared in surprise. 'That's a pretty strange-looking bazooka,' he said.

'No, it's a pretty *impressive*-looking bazooka . . . for a beginner,' said Whippet proudly.

Simon turned to Knuckles. 'How did they build it so fast?'

'Time works in weird ways here in

Comic. If the story needs something in a hurry, it might appear instantly, like Duster just did in *The Silent Kite*. Or, if you need a little drama, time might slow. Like the stampede. They should have reached us hours ago, but here we all are. Alive and kicking and preparing for the big finale.'

Lucy was studying her construction. She pointed to a section of exposed wiring.

'We're not quite done. We've a weak connection point here. These wires need insulation but we ran out of plastic.'

Simon looked down at the action figure he was still holding. It looked to be the perfect size. He tossed the toy to Lucy, who

caught it with a smile and set to work feeding the wiring through the figure.

'Even your *merchandise* saves the day,' said Simon to Knuckles.

'Okay,' said Whippet, 'problem time. Where is the **PANEL**?'

Knuckles walked up the valley a short way, then stopped. He pulled the sleeve of his coat over his fist and began to do a strange rubbing movement in the air. But it wasn't the air. A smudge of white appeared before them. The smudge got bigger and brighter.

'You painted over it,' said Whippet in delight. 'That is some camouflage!'

'Okay,' said Simon, 'so we push this machine through the PANEL and use it to close it behind us.'

'That won't work. This is a Comic construction. It will only work here, in Comic,' said Knuckles.

Simon swallowed. 'But how do we destroy the PANEL and get home? Someone is going to have to stay and fire this thing . . . which means they'll be trapped.'

'Correct. You three are leaving. Right now,' said Knuckles, placing his hands on Simon's and Whippet's shoulders and gently steering them towards the PANEL.

Simon twisted free and turned to face Knuckles.

'No! Dad, you can't do this!' he yelled.

'I can and I must. It's my responsibility. It always has been. It's the only solution.'

'But . . . But what will I say to Ruby? What will I tell Mum?' said Simon.

'Not to worry. You have nothing to fear. I know *another* way back, but it will take time. I promise you, son, this machine won't be the end of me,' said Knuckles.

He hugged Simon to his chest.

'And besides, I won't be alone,' he added.

Simon pulled away. Something had brushed his leg.

It was Gubbin, and he was wrapped around Knuckles's ankles.

Lucy knelt down next to her pet.

'Now, how on *earth* did YOU follow us here?' said Lucy in amazement, before looking up at Knuckles. 'Gubbin comes from Comic, right? Did you give her to my grandfather . . . to give to me?' she said.

Knuckles looked silently at the strange creature for a while.

'I knew your parents, Lucy,' he said eventually, 'and their disappearance was unfathomable. Not that it helps, but I spent years searching for them in this place. Your mother didn't just design my gadgets, she knew all about Comic. So I thought . . . you know . . . maybe they came here. Maybe they got lost. And you were so small . . . I wanted to do something good for you. Give you something positive. But honestly though, Gubbin chose *you*. This fuzzy boy has got more lives than a cat,' said Knuckles.

Gubbin jumped up onto his shoulder.

'But now it looks like he wants to keep me company. I couldn't hope for a luckier charm,' said Knuckles.

Gubbin blinked slowly at Lucy. Lucy flicked her gaze from the little creature to Knuckles.

'My parents,' she whispered, 'if they are in here . . . if you believe it . . . if there's even the smallest, tiniest chance . . .'

'I never stopped looking, and I don't intend to now,' said Knuckles tenderly.

Lucy swallowed, nodded stiffly, then grabbed Simon and Whippet and began to head towards the **PANEL**. Simon tried to resist, but it was no good. A determined Lucy was far stronger than she looked.

Knuckles turned on the Eradicator. The metal expanded as energy coursed through the machine. A symphony of sounds overlapped each other as the contraption fought to hold itself together

against the power that was building in its heart.

Simon was crying silently now.

'Dad . . . don't! Don't!'

'This isn't *The End*, son,' Knuckles yelled over the rising, wailing din. 'This is Comic, remember? This is just . . .

To Be Continued!

There was light everywhere. It was flowing from the Eradicator, flowing from the PANEL. Lucy slowly counted to three, then launched herself, and the boys, forwards.

CHAPTER 22

UNLIKELY SAVIOURS

They landed on stone, which hurt a lot more than their arrival in Comic. Simon struggled to get to his feet and made a desperate lunge for the **PANEL**. Whippet caught hold of his friend's leg and held on tight, and in doing so saved his life, for a second later the **PANEL** began to buckle. It writhed and twisted. Ribbons of light

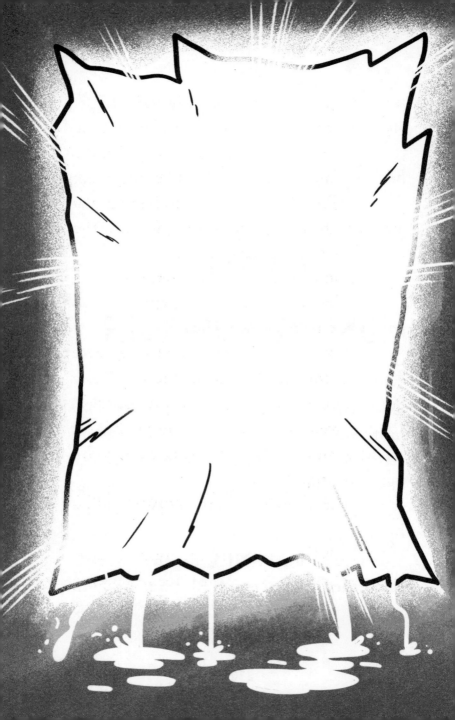

peeled away from the original shape, slapping the floor all around and melting the stone where they landed. Lucy and the boys scrambled back to avoid getting fried.

The **PANEL** continued to hang in the air as it fought desperately against the effects of the Eradicator.

Simon turned to face the dungeon.

Things in the real world appeared to have gone from bad to worse.

T-Rex and Captain Armstrong were standing with their arms in the air. Ernie Shufflebottom was pointing a strange tube-shaped weapon directly at them. Buster stood beside his desk looking even more miserable than before.

'What are you doing NOW?' yelled Lucy.

'Much like yourselves, it appears these two heroes decided to return. Seems they did not trust me when I said I'd look after you.'

'They were right! And that's my original prototype Eradicator,' snapped Lucy. 'So YOU stole it!'

'Well, it needed a little tweaking so it wouldn't explode, but it's really a marvellous machine. Well done, dear. Disintegrates runaway monsters in *moments*. Like that Squid up in the tower.'

Lucy marched up to her grandfather.

'This is all your fault – everything! I've spent years fighting bizarre, deadly, non-sensical creatures because YOU were

bringing them to earth. And then you go and push my friends into another dimension! We might share a surname, but as far as I'm concerned we are no longer related!'

'Don't get carried away, Lucy. Everyone's doing just fine. As you've somehow managed to destroy my **PANEL**, and as a consequence my entire comic empire, why don't we forget all this, call it even and move on?'

Lucy threw her arms up in despair.

'Simon's dad is lost in another world; T-Rex and Armstrong and all these monsters are stuck on Earth; you've been putting the town and the whole world in danger for decades, all in order to sell *COMICS* . . . and you think we're *EVEN*?!'

Ernie thought about it for a second, then shrugged. 'Well, desperate times . . .' he began.

'. . . call for *Danica* measures,' said a calm voice from the back of the dungeon.

They all turned as one. Danica and Ruby were standing at the top of the amphi-theatre stairs.

'Who . . . ? Who are *you*?' said Ernie in disbelief.

'Whippet's girlfriend, Lucy and Simon's friend, Ruby's babysitter . . . and the girl who brings your story to an end,' said Danica.

'Haha!' Ernie laughed. 'I've faced horrors from a parallel realm and you think

I'm going to be scared of a small girl?'

Danica lifted Ruby up until she was
level with a large lever connected to the wall.

'Your granddaughter is Lucy Shufflebottom. You most certainly should be scared
of girls. Now let's find out if your monstrous
herd has appreciated its time in captivity.'

And with that Ruby
yanked the lever down and
a hundred cage doors
flew open.

The colour drained from Ernie's face.

The monsters were loose. ALL the monsters. And judging from the scrambling, seething manner in which they fled their cages, they were very, very glad to be out.

Simon, Whippet and Lucy dived for cover beneath Buster's drawing board, as

T-Rex sprinted up the stairs, grabbed Danica and Ruby, and pulled them towards the lift – the only direction the monsters were not headed.

Captain Armstrong ran to the table and shielded the children from the rolling, ravenous mass of monstrosities. Buster scrambled forward in a desperate attempt to join them, but was knocked to the ground by a wriggling creature shaped like an electric eel.

'Back, back, all of you,' shouted Ernie, firing his Eradicator frantically in all directions. Luckily he hit nothing but air.

Then everything went a little nuts.

Simon could see only glimpses of the action

from where they were
crouched, but Ernie seemed
to be lifted physically off his
feet by the rampaging horde
and carried directly
backwards towards the
hole of the collapsing
PANEL. As streams of
uncontrolled energy
whipped around him,
Lucy's grand-father
was heard to
utter a final
f u r i o u s
proclamation.
*'This is
not The
End ...'*

'This is just . . . *To Be Continued*,' whispered Simon.

Then Ernie was gone, and the monsters were gone, and the **PANEL** was gone. It folded in on itself and with a last loud *R-R-RIP*, it simply ceased to be.

The room was silent as the survivors climbed down the steps or got to their feet and gathered together in the centre of the dungeon.

Simon stared at the patch of bare wall where the panel had been. It looked quite ordinary but he'd never seen anything worse in all his life.

Captain Armstrong knelt beside Buster, who was lying dazed on the floor. Ironically, he had been saved from sharing Ernie's fate by the chain that Ernie had used to tie him to his desk. Then the Captain moved to Lucy's side and lay a large gentle hand on her shoulder. She didn't shake it off.

Whippet looked at the girl beside him. His hand, working on automatic, found Danica's.

'Er, that was . . . that . . . wow. But how did you even know we were in trouble?'

Danica grinned. 'Ever since our camping trip to Wailing Wood I've tried to stay close to you boys. Making friends with Ruby was easy and, unlike you two, she's very happy to share her secrets. Ruby told me all about the Snotticus, but it wasn't until I spoke to Simon on the phone earlier, when he said you were absolutely, categorically NOT in trouble, that I realised you needed help.'

'Ah,' said Whippet. 'Clever.'

He looked down at their hands.

'I'm not sure how I feel about this. I've, um, never had a girlfriend,' he admitted.

'Well, we can work on that,' said Danica, and planted a gentle kiss on a very surprised Whippet's cheek.

Ruby shuffled over to Simon. He had sat himself down on Buster's chair. His head was in his hands. She reached up and hugged him so tightly he actually yelped.

'Please don't be mad that I came to find you,' she whispered.

Simon gave her the biggest cuddle of her life.

'I'm not. Believe me, I'm not . . . You don't know how much I needed this,' he told her.

He couldn't even begin to explain to Ruby what had happened to their dad. It would have to wait for another day. For now, they simply held each other.

After all, if he was right, they had just saved the world.

The guilty had got their just deserts.

And *almost* everyone was there to see it happen.

CHAPTER 23

DRAWING A NEW DAWN

It was agreed that the police should probably *not* be called. Without Ernie or the **PANEL** or any monsters, there really wasn't much of a crime to report.

Buster seemed to be in shock as they unchained his leg, and as they took the lift upstairs to the library he babbled endlessly about **PANELS**. The loss of Ernie had

obviously hit him harder than he'd care to admit. Lucy's grandfather may have lost his way, but they had been friends and partners for a lifetime.

Buster had refused to leave the dungeon until he'd gathered his final comic pages. Simon presumed they were a sort of memento. Something to remember Ernie by. The last comic they would ever make together. Never to be printed.

It was almost tragic.

But Simon was wrong.

Outside, in the cool evening air,

Armstrong informed them that Buster would be coming to live with him at the Shipshape Shop for a while, until he was feeling better. As they set off with T-Rex in tow, Buster suddenly stopped and shook the pages clutched in his hands.

He turned back to the children.

'For what it's worth, Lucy, I'm really very sorry it finished like this. Ernie took

the wrong path at the end, but he didn't
start out that way . . . Perhaps you'll do
better,' he said.

Lucy glared at him. There was hurt in
her eyes.

'What do you mean?' she murmured.

'The Castle. The Empire. **FREAKY** and
FEARLESS. As Ernie's only living relative, it's
all now yours,' said Buster.

Lucy stood very still. She turned to the
castle. Like seeing the bright colours of
Comic, she blinked, looking at it as if for
the first time.

Buster beckoned to Whippet and Simon
and they stepped closer.

'Ernie knew what you both were.
The TELLER and the CREATOR. I think
he was less worried that you'd discover the
secret of our storytelling success than
he was of what you might eventually

become. He feared you as the *competition*. See, you boys don't need to copy good ideas. You make them up from scratch.'

Buster thrust the folded comic pages into Simon's hands.

'Want to know why the comic was delayed this week? Ernie found out I'd been trying to hide messages in the pages of **FREAKY**! I started this week's, but I never got to finish the strip. Your story's not over, Simon . . .'

Simon looked down. The ragged pile of paper was, in fact, a brand-new issue of **FREAKY** . . . the only known copy in existence. The last issue likely to ever be made.

The gang stood in the driveway beneath a pale moon.

Simon lowered the comic. He turned to Whippet, who'd been reading the pages over his shoulder.

'Remember the cover of last week's?' said Simon. 'It was a BLACK rectangle. Like the **PANEL**, but not *white* . . . it was black. The **PANEL** was bright and light, but the portal that Jonas stepped through is all shades of darkness. Is Buster trying to tell us there's *another* way in? Another **PANEL**?'

Simon's voice was filled with hope, but when he turned around to question Buster, he discovered that he'd already left.

The two boys stared at the double-page spread in silence. Then Whippet threw his arm around his friend's shoulder and plucked the comic from his hand.

'Mossy, your dad has been adventuring in Comic pretty much your whole life. He's Knuckles, and he's got Gubbin by his side. **PANEL** or no **PANEL**, he'll find a way back, I'm sure of it. You never know, he might even find Lucy's parents.'

Simon gave a small laugh. How he hoped it was all true.

'Tonight, for now, let's treat *this* thing as a comic. Just printed pages, written and drawn for kids like us to enjoy,' said Whippet.

'That works for me,' said Simon.

'Plus, we've got bigger problems to worry about. We're seriously LATE! Our mums are going to come looking for us pretty soon, so we should probably start acting normal.'

Lucy appeared from nowhere and clapped them both on the shoulder.

'"Normal" is what happens to other people,' said Lucy. 'Besides, I've an offer that you'll find extremely interesting, and it is anything *but* normal.'

Simon and Whippet turned to face their friend. She raised one hand in mock greeting.

'Hi, I'm Lucy Shufflebottom, action heroine, explorer extraordinaire, survivor of inter-dimensional world-saving escapades, and the new owner of both Castle Fearless and the **FREAKY** and **FEARLESS** comic empires. Due to a recent staff shortage, I seem to be in rather desperate need of both a new writer and an artist.'

The boys held their breath.

'If you two think of anyone suitable,' said Lucy, as she turned on her heel and began to march in a comedy fashion back towards the castle, 'do be sure to send me their details. A good BOSS is always on the lookout for story-TELLERs and talented CREATORS.'

She turned back and waved at them.

'Well, goodnight!'

The boys grinned at one another, then bolted after her.

'Wait,' laughed Simon. 'Come back here!'

'Stop!' shouted Whippet.

And with that, the boys charged headlong towards a future that was yet to be written.

Or drawn.

THE END

ROBIN ETHERINGTON, as one half of The Etherington Brothers, has written three graphic novels that have been nominated for an array of awards. He has also produced comic stories for bestselling brands like Star Wars, Transformers, Wallace and Gromit, The Dandy, Kung Fu Panda and How to Train Your Dragon as well as writing for animation and film. Robin regularly tours schools and book festivals with events in the UK and abroad. Through energetic, laughter-filled Q&A sessions he loves to share his passion for reading, writing, art and the power of imagination. *Freaky & Fearless* is his first novel series.

JAN BIELECKI has studied both comics and illustration and has co-created two critically acclaimed graphic novels in Swedish. He is also a prolific children's book illustrator and his work has been published in Sweden, the UK and France. He has illustrated the *Wrestling Trolls* series for Hot Key Books. He would rather draw than describe himself:

Piccadilly

P R E S S

Thank you for choosing a Piccadilly Press book.

If you would like to know more about our authors, our books or if you'd just like to know what we're up to, you can find us online.

www.piccadillypress.co.uk

You can also find us on:

We hope to see you soon!